Your Truth was Told, This is Mine

I know "kindness" and "forgiveness" will take us anywhere we want to go.

Dorothy Jenkins

ACKNOWLEDGMENTS

Unconditional Love, Kindness, and Support

* Lisa: "last born" my baby girl Her husband: John

* Their sons: Jonathon and Jayson

* Nathan: only son: his wife Kisha Their sons: Nathan, Amuri, and Ameir Vincent: my husband

* Gilbert and Sarah: uncle and aunt Earline and Mars: aunts

* Sandford and Gwen: cousins Lucillie: sister-in-law

* Betty and John: aunt and uncle Shaneque: niece

* Lucillie: cousin

* May: aunt

* Sandy: friend

TABLE OF CONTENTS

Be a blessing, this book can be purchased from the link below. The Ebook is $2.99 and the Paperback is $9.95.

https://www.amazon.com/Your-Truth-Told-This-Mine/dp/B095GCZMMX/ref=cm_cr_arp_d_product_top?ie=UTF8

Be blessed and Thank you.

CHAPTER 1

MERCY, COMPASSION AND LOVING KINDNESS

Common Sense

When I was growing up, I thought everyone in the world had 'common sense.' Now I know better. You see, I lived on a farm of twenty acres with my grandparents, and they always told me everyone had common sense. They also told me there will be some who choose not to use it, not realizing that it is a part of our intelligence. Mama grand, which was what we called our grandmother, said when growing up, we must be somewhat intelligent to help us recognize that we have common sense and should utilize it. My first indication of common sense growing up was when family or friends would come over to our home, and my grandparents would greet them with a smile, hand shake, and hug. Most of the time, I would be standing right beside her or somewhere nearby. She would tell them to have a seat and ask them if they wanted a glass of water or something to eat. Mama grand was always so very kind to everyone. She would say, "if you grow up with kindness in your heart, and as you grow into an adult using your kindness along with your common sense, it will tell you we must go out and obtain an education, and I assure you will live a "Prosperous Life" with a lot of happiness. What was so amazing to me is when people came over, she would say to them, are you hungry and before they could answer, she would request they have a seat. While the guests were sitting, she would go into the kitchen, make a fire in the wood stove, and cook a full course meal. In less than an hour and while she is doing this, the

1

people and family would be sitting down, talking and laughing with my grandfather. The expressions on their faces would indicate they were having a joyful time.

Common Sense

The same attitude would follow everyone into the dining area. I remember mama grand saying to me, "when you grow up with kindness in your heart, we would be able to successfully get along with most of the reasonable human being in this world." That left me believing that everyone has common sense, but I know now they may not use it But to this day, it's amazing to me when we have something so unique, why wouldn't they use it.

Dorothy Mae Pickens Jenkins

Amplified Bible (Zondervan)

Luke: C2, V47
And all who heard Him were astonished and overwhelmed with bewildered wonder at His intelligence and understanding and His replies.

Job: C6, V14
To him who is about to faint and despair, kindness is due from his friend, least he forsake the fear of the Almighty.

Proverbs: C31, V26
She opens her mouth in skillful and godly Wisdom, and on her tongue is the law of kindness [giving counsel and instruction].

2

Deuteronomy: C29, V9

Therefore keep the words of this covenant and do them that you may deal paisley and prosper in all that you do.

Common Sense

Mrs. Earlee was one of these people who had such kindness in her heart for others. Especially for wives and husbands until she finds herself making sure he or she is being treated fairly by whoever was involved. No matter how complex the person or persons was and still is, emotions would run high, low, and sometimes in between. And that would cause a lot of conflict and confusion when the persons you are trying to protect did not ever, never speak up for themselves. The person wouldn't know what to do or say to his wife because they don't know how, but I find that is not entirely true. They were simply afraid too, and they didn't want to deal with conflict. So unfairly, they stand back and let the savior-faire, get their emotion torn apart.

And that person or persons become emotional stress to the limit, because in the meantime he or she was too insecure. And not at all concerned about what this would do to her, the Savoir, but he had no doubt whether she or he could handle it. He just didn't think or care about what it did to her emotional and physical well being. Through it all, she managed to keep her dignity but almost destroy her emotion and well being of the marriage. Now you ask why did this happen because he was and still is (insecure), but at least he is standing. It's a little, but he's standing and what happened to her? They are still standing, but their foundation has been weakened because they allowed themselves to lose their marriage because they were too insecure about fighting for it. They should not have trusted anyone to save something that was so important as their marriage. He was and is her husband, but at the time, she was married to herself. Why did her husband stand by and let his wife be ridiculed because? It was drilled into him that she was inferior to him, and he was taught never to trust anyone but his mother. And if he showed any trust toward the wife, she would become infelicitous with outrageous pride. And she would say she is inferior to you anyway, so she sets out to maliciously destroy her. But she didn't see she was destroying her own son, or is it she just didn't care.

Dorothy Mae Pickens Jenkins

Amplified Bible (Zandervan)

Job: C6, V14

14) To him who is about to faint and despair, kindness is due from his friend, lest he forsake the fear of the Almighty.

Psalm: C141, V1, V3

1) Lord, I call upon You; hasten to me Give ear to my voice when I cry to You.

3) Set a guard, O Lord, before my mouth; keep watch at the door of my lips.

James: C4, V1

1) WHAT LEADS to strife (discord and feuds) and how do conflicts (quarrels and fightings) originate among you? Do they not arise from your sensual desires that are ever warring in your bodily members?

Common Sense

Annie found in her life it is very difficult to meet good quality, kind, caring people. And when she did, she cherishes it, and it filled her with gratitude. And she went forward, hoping she could make other people feel like she felt. Sometimes when meeting people, they don't come across as accepting, caring people. In Annie's experience, she had not met many people that were loving and kind. So she was overwhelmed, and her heart was pierced with kindness, and it remained with her forever. Her thoughts were that she hoped that she could continue to meet people with kind qualities. As a part of our society, she would teach our children and others to be kind and sympathetic. At this particular time, she was a working professional and worked toward becoming an entrepreneur. She was very committed to her plan, and yes, there were stumbling blocks, ditch digging against her, but that didn't stop her; she kept holding on through all of it. Annie could see knowing this family made her want to care about people even more than she already did. And when meeting this young lady and her family, Annie became so grateful for the opportunity.

To have known someone of her caliber, strength, power and goaloriented toward a successful future. For this is a very prosperous family that. Annie wholes dear to her heart. Annie believes she will meet other families, and she's going to trust herself to make good, sound, confident decisions. In Annie's experience, there are deceiving people right there in her face, but this young woman kept her confidence and steadfastness. Through it, all and remained calm, constructive and professional with no animosity. Annie learned when she saw this young woman putting her life into existence to make sure it was for the better good of all. And in the process of obtaining success, she also became a homeowner.

Dorothy Mae Pickens Jenkins

Amplified Bible (Zondervan)

Romans: C15, V5

5) Now may the God Who gives the power of patient endurance (steadfastness) and Who supplies encouragement, grant you to live in such mutual harmony and such full sympathy with one another, in accord with Christ Jesus.

Psalm: C94, V8

8) Consider and understand you stupid ones among the people! And you [self-confident] fools, when will you become wise?

Psalm: C92, V14

14) [Growing in grace] they shall still bring forth fruit in old age, they shall be full of sap [of spiritual vitality] and [rich in the] venture [of trust, love, and contentment].

Proverbs: C8, V35

35) For whoever finds me [Wisdom] finds life and draws forth and obtains favor from the Lord.

Common Sense

Lena said she has met some of the most kind people she has met in her entire life. Meaning they are good people and they stand by their word. The reality of their life is the goodness of how they live and treat each other and other people. That is very rare in today's society, and I am so fortunate to have met people who are genuine in who they are

6

and what they do. People like these are always looking for someone to be kind to even when they are in a very difficult place in their own life. That is what makes them so unique, and the uniqueness of them will reach many people throughout the world. And make us become better and kinder people so we may teach our children about the goodness of humility. And that is one way this world will become better. It is as if we as human beings need to start caring more about the feelings of others than our personal selves. Lena personally knows only a handful of young women that are true to their convictions. And standing firmly on them no matter what someone else is saying or doing. These people are to be admired and commended by our society, and hopeful we can learn from them. And let what we have learned spread throughout our schools and colleges. And if there were more people like them we could start to have people like them in professional high places. Then the world could be ruled by a kind and caring people rather than your basic rich people.

Who only cares about the top of the shelf, not the bottom or the middle. But we have to know if you don't care for the bottom or the middle, the foundation will fall. And that's what's happened to our society as a whole today. We need more kind caring people to put more emphasis on the feelings of others. And start thinking and making decisions to enhance our society by making contributions to society from the bottom, not from the top down; if we continue to treat the symptoms from the top down, then the bottom and the middle will become infected and fall. Then what happens is we have to start all over again when they simply could have given the care that everyone needed from the beginning. It would not have gotten infected and fallen in, if they had taken the time to give the average care at the proper time. So you see, it goes right back to our convictions being genuine in our convictions and standing by each other. And that is the reality of our genuine world and the understanding of it.

Dorothy Mae Pickens Jenkins

Amplified Bible (Zondervan)

Psalm: C37, V30
30) The mouth of the [uncompromisingly] righteous utters wisdom, and his tongue speaks with justice.

Psalm: C111, V4
4) He has made His wonderful works to be remembered: the Lord is gracious, merciful, and full of loving compassion.

Psalm:C115, V1
1) NOT TO us, O Lord, not to us but to Your name give glory, for Your mercy and loving kindness and for the sake of Your truth and faithfulness!

Psalm:C145, V8
8) The Lord is gracious and full of compassion, slow to anger and abounding in mercy and loving kindness.

Common Sense

Victoria is a very unique young woman with her very own behavior temperament. She makes us feel at ease, with gentle kindness, compassion, and loyalty. We could miss understanding her goodness as a performance, but it is clearly not. She is a very pleasing individual with no devious intent in her heart for anyone. She is very family-oriented, and common sense significant to her self worth. And believing she can help others to commonly achieve the comfort of life for themselves. The steadfastness and endurance and her faith kept her to the truth. And the ways of the world, her faith carry with her every day of her life. And translating it to anyone and everyone she came in contact with, good or bad. She has such a beautiful spirit about herself regardless of who or what she involved herself in. And whatever circumstances she encounters, she handles it with dignity and always keeps her composure. Believe me, she has dealt with some people that were totally insane and still is, but she handles it with the hands of a complete professional. And again, with no physical contact, violence or dirty words. What I am trying to convey to you all is that a quiet person is not always as the old saying said. You better watch those quiet ones; they are more dangerous than the average angered person with the probability of doing something unorthodox. These people have excellent communication skills and above-average successful integrity, understanding, responsibility, commitment and loyalties to all people of our society, and they are very spiritual people. As mama grand would say, she's an old soul meaning she is just the one to pursue And she is left with the satisfaction of helping someone through an ordeal with compassion, words, and understanding. Her steadfastness and endurance and faith will remain in her well-reserved soul. We must stop and listen. She will teach you how to obtain faith and follow the goodness of the word and never be without it. This young lady's decision making is phenomenal; that's why she is such access to all people. To help them become all they want in their lifetime. And leave a quality of caring and hard work with all our generations to come. She is one of the most gentle, generous people that we have had the pleasure of being in her company. Professional and as an individual, we need people like her to help society to become a better place for our grandchildren to make a better place for their children. I would think now the question that's weighing on your mind is what kind of prudential does she have. She has a high school diploma; that is what is so unique about this young lady. That she's able to work in this capacity with such successful achievements, she relied on her common sense and the strength of her faith. So she may bless others with the benefit of her hard work.

Dorothy Mae Pickens Jenkins

Amplified Bible (Zondervan)

Philippians: C4, V6

6) Do not fret or have any anxiety about anything, but in every circumstance and in everything, by prayer and petition (t definite requests), with thanksgiving, continue to make your wants known to God.

Titus: C3, V1

REMIND PEOPLE to be submissive to [their] magistrates and authorities, to be obedient, to be prepared and willing to do say upright and honorable work.

Psalm: C111, V4 & V7

4) He has made His wonderful works to be remembered: the Lord is gracious, merciful, and full of loving compassion.

7) The works of His hands are [absolute] truth and justice [faithful and right]: and all His decrees and precepts are sure (fixed, established, and trustworthy).

Common Sense

Mr Amos recognized we need to have mercy for folk; some of us don't have kindness and compassion in our heart or recognize we should give mercy to each other. It's freely given to us every day of our lives, so if it's freely given to us, can't you all see giving mercy to each other would be a good thing too? There are times we are not going to know what to say or do, just say Mercy You see, back in the seventies, she was a divorced single black woman raising her children. She didn't realize how much she depended on. Mercy during those times. The only other person she could depend on to help to raise her baby girl was her (twelve-year-old son), he was the middle child. The children had to listen and pay close attention to what she said to them, and do what she told them, and asked them to. Because their well being depended on them doing exactly what the mother said and how she said it, and when she wanted it done. That is how they were able to survive; basically, they were good children; they had to be good children. Because the mother went to school part-time and worked full time. The fifteen-year-old child wasn't a bad child; she just wanted to be grown and in charge. So that meant the (twelve years old) son had to be in charge and follow his mother's instructions. As Mama grand said, you have to know how to follow instructions, use your common sense, cross all your T's and dot all your I's. And don't leave no stones unturned, and you will succeed, and they did. She has three beautiful, grown, independent, responsible, and successful children. Those adult children are allowing Mercy into their lives every day.

Dorothy Mae Pickens Jenkins

Amplified Bible (Zondervan)

Romans C9, V16

16) so then [God's is not a question of human will and human effort, but of God's Mercy It depends not on one's own willingness nor on his strenuous exertion as in running a race God's having mercy on him.

Hebrew C2, V13

13) And again He says, My trust and assured reliance and confident hope shall be fixed in Him And yet again, Here I I and the children whom God has given Me.

Jonah C2, V8

8) Those who pay regard to false, useless, And worthless idols forsake their own [Source mercy and loving-kindness.

Genesis C39, V21

21) But the Lord was with Joseph, and showed him mercy and lovingkindness and gave him favor in the sight of the warden of the prison.

Common Sense

Al tried to live a faultless life style; he was very confident and forever persuasive in knowing his place in life. Confident in knowing his word is all anyone needed to feel loved. Confident within himself and in the world he lives in. The ingredients that were in him was a delicious fresh loaf of baked bread. When you start to eat it, you will never get enough of it. And being around him, it was as if they became a more vibrant and caring person. An independent person feeling as if he has got it all together. And he loves every moment of the life he has made for himself.

Because of his teaching to others and the way he would talk and treat them with the utmost respect. There was no time that you needed him, and he wasn't there. That was very comforting to all that knew him; that was his way of life looking after others. More than he did himself, this man would produce small miracles within a human being and throughout the community. You asked if he was a family man, yes he was, and he had a compassionate heart about him. Even if you weren't family, he made you feel like family and treated you just that way. He had a sense of decency about himself; you might feel like a human being, you don't want to listen to what he had to say. But he had his way about himself; you would start to pay attention to what he is saying and for his love for people. It would make all the sense in the world, even where a child could understand. He would always leave you with the effects of feeling complete, safe and loved.

Dorothy Mae Pickens Jenkins

Amplified Bible (Zondervan)

Jude: C1, V20

20) But you, behold, build yourselves up [founded] on your most holy faith [make progress, rise like an edifice higher and higher], praying in the Holy Spirit:

Psalm: C119, V90

90) Your faithfulness is from generation to generation: You have established the earth and it stands fast.

Psalm: C117, V2

2) For His mercy and loving-kindness are great toward us, and the truth and faithfulness of the Lord endure forever. Praise the Lord!

(Hallelujah).

Isaiah: C33, V6

6)And there shall be stability in your times an abundance of salvation wisdom and knowledge the reverent fear and worship of the lord is your treasure and his.

Common Sense

Mr. Austin said now that we are willing to receive so much from using our common sense, by listening, it's time for us to give back with grace in our heart. Giving loving kindness is being grateful and thankful for what we have learned. Our bodies may not feel like giving much as we know we should; that's normal. But only we know to endure and give help to our sisters and brothers In helping each other, we will gain knowledge from each other. Doing this together, we share a common bond with how society works.

Dorothy Mae Pickens Jenkins

Amplified Bible (Zondervan)

Isaiah C1, V19

19) If ye be willing and obedient, ye shall eat the good of the land.

Luke C22, V42

42) saying Father, if thou be willing, remove this cup from me, nevertheless not my will, but thine, be done.

Job C6, V12

12) Is my strength and endurance that of stones? Or is my flesh made of bronze?

Psalm C19, V9

9) The [reverent] fear of the Lord is clean, enduring forever, the ordinances of the Lord are true and righteous altogether.

Common Sense

Mr. Bill said, this is my "future" Father!! thank you, thank you Father. Thank you for this day. I finally have forgiven all the people in my life that have hurt or disrespected me. "You Father said," God promised me through his word we can and will live our lives in peace, with loving-kindness. It is essential that I remained myself and continue to be a peaceful, loving, caring person. And still enjoying being a peacemaker for all hurting and none hurting people. With love, moral, integrity, and obedience is the key to a caring loving stronger generation.

Dorothy Mae Pickens Jenkins

Amplified Bible (Zondervan)

Psalm C35, V27

27) Let those who favor my righteous cause and have pleasure in My uprightness shout for joy and be glad and say continually, Let the Lord be magnified. Who takes pleasure and prosperity of His servant.

II Corinthians C3, V12

12) Since we have such [glorious] hope (such joyful and confident expectation), we speak very freely and openly and fearlessly.

Numbers C14, V18

18) The Lord is long-suffering and slow to anger, and abundant in

mercy and loving-kindness, forgiving iniquity and transgression: but He will by no means clear the guilty, visiting the iniquity of the fathers upon the children, upon the third and fourth generation [Exod, 34:6, 7].

Numbers C6, V26
26) The Lord lift up His [approving] countenance upon you and give you peace (tranquility of heart and life continually).

Common Sense

Mrs. Spooks said love is a graceful privilege to be generous of giving kindness, mercy, and goodness. Living a quiet peaceful life working at having no strife in our life. Keeping your heart in good agreement, talking with whomever is in or around us in our lives. Staying calm and maintaining gentleness, kindness and loving relationships.

Dorothy Mae Pickens Jenkins

Amplified Bible (Zondervan)

Job C22, V21
21) Acquaint yourself now with Him [agree with God and show yourself to be conformed to His will] and be at peace: by that [you shall prosper and great] good shall come to you.

Psalm C34, V14
14) Depart from evil and do good, seek, inquire for, and crave peace and pursue (go after).

Psalm C84, V11 & V12
For the Lord God is a Sun and Shield: the Lord bestows [present] grace

and favor and [future] glory [honor, splendor, and heavenly bliss)! No good thing will He withhold from those who walk uprightly.

Common Sense

O Lord of hosts, blessed (happy, fortunate, to be envied) is the man who trusts in You [learning and believing on You, committing all and confidently looking to You, and that without fear or misgiving!!

Maydale said we must have a desired to care for other people; our heart should feel it is necessary. And a requirement of us to look after each other. Making sure we are useful, sharing and caring human beings without allowing it to become extremely difficult to understand. Stop allowing yourself to have a poverty-stricken mind. What is a poverty stricken mind? When you have a mind, but there's nothing there And you refuse to use it positively.

Dorothy Mae Pickens Jenkins

Amplified Bible (Zondervan)

Romans C12, V13
Contribute to the needs of God's people [sharing in necessities of the saints], pursue the practice of hospitality.

Acts C20, V34
34) You yourselves know personally that these hands ministered to my own needs and those [of the persons] who were with me.

Romans C12R, V17V19
17) Repay no one evil for evil but take thought for what is honest and proper and noble [aiming to be above reproach] in the sight of

everyone [Prov 20:22].

19) Beloved, never avenge yourselves, but leave the way open for [God's] wrath: for it is written.

Vengeance is Mine I will repay (require), says the Lord [Deut 32:35].

Common Sense

Alexis said mothers, fathers, aunts, uncles, and extended families, our children, grandchildren and all of the generations to come. They are in big trouble, they need us so what are we going to do? Are we going to sit or stand around like mannequins doing nothing for our children, looking at them becoming mannequins themselves? Don't you see what is happening to them? They are waiting on us to tell them and show them what to do. The children are trying to do something good with their lives don't have parents or grandparents to help them.

Because over half of us are sitting around saying we don't know what to do, a good place to start is to let them know we love them. And teaching them about the rights, wrongs, and life of giving lovingkindness and showing our children that we love them by responding to their needs. Our children need to feel valued and cared for. If we don't get off our behinds and convince our children that we love and care for them. We are going to lose another generation of our beautiful babies, but don't you see we have to teach them how to get theirs, the right way within half the time in which we did All our children want is an opportunity to live a good life for themselves, their children and their extended families. We must make them see, you have to do it the right way. And we, as parents, it is a necessity to be accessible to our children when they need us.

Please, our beautiful children need us and let us allow ourselves to teach them to love, respect, and care for each other. And in the end, I promise you, their life will become just what we wanted, all under the umbrella of love and respect.

Dorothy Mae Pickens Jenkins

Amplified Bible (Zondervan)

Psalm: C37, V3 & V4

Trust (lean on, rely on, and be confident) in the Lord and do good, so shall you dwell in the land and feed surely on His faithfulness, and truly you shall be fed.

Delight yourself also in the Lord, and He will give you the desires and secret petitions of your heart.

Hebrews C10, V23 & V24

So let us seize and hold fast and retain without wavering the hope we cherish and confess and our acknowledgement of it, for He Who promised is reliable (sure) and faithful to His word.

And let us consider and give attentive, continuous care to watching over one another studying how we may stir up (stimulate and incite) to love and helpful deeds and noble activities.

Common Sense

Mr. Wes said let us talk about faith, which is something we have to have within us. And believe in faith just as we believe in our common sense. We have to have common sense enough to know it is a necessity, that we recognize without faith, there is no successful future for us. And that we know it is essential for us to improve ourselves beyond just common sense. We must comprehend that we have to allow ourselves to become educated, as entrepreneurs, and create business for ourselves. As (Mama Grand) said we are prudent, and merciful people so we must do this for ourselves and success will spread through our neighborhoods, towns, cities, and states. I assure you when we see the neighborhoods thriving so will our children that's a promise we must make to ourselves and become prosperous.

Dorothy Mae Pickens Jenkins

Amplified Bible (Zondervan)

II Corinthians C1, V24

24) Not that we have dominion [over you] and lord it over your faith, but [rather that work with you fellow laborers [to promote] your joy, for in[your] faith (in your strong and welcome convention or belief that Jesus is the Messiah, through. When we obtain eternal salvation in the kingdom of God) you stand Firm.

II Corinthians C8, V7, V8, & V9

Now as you abound and excel and are at the front in everything in faith, in expressing yourselves, in knowledge, in all zeal, and in your love for us_[see to it that you come to the front now and] abound and excel in this gracious work [of almsgiving] also.

I give this not as an order [to dictate to you], but to prove, by [pointing out] the zeal of others, the sincerity of your [own] love also.

For you are becoming progressively acquainted with recognizing more strongly and clearly the grace of our Lord Jesus Christ (His kindness, His gracious generosity, His undeserved favor and spiritual blessing), [in] that though. He was very] rich, yet for your sakes he became very] poor in order that by His poverty you might become enriched (abundantly supplied).

Common Sense

Mrs. Daisy said, have you ever heard of the old saying, give someone enough rope they will hang themselves. Well, this person did exactly that; she hasn't the inability or ingredients to be kind and loving to people. She is a very deceptive person, always trying to call her bluff on someone else. She is a very deceiving person from the way she acts; we would assume she doesn't really know the fundamentals of life. It is as if she thinks the basic essentials of life do not apply to her. She wanted to be respected, but she didn't want to give respect. She is a person that only cares about herself and abolishes everyone else's beliefs. She is incapable of achieving a caring and loving relationship with others. I have seen her be very persistent in what she wants, but then after she gets what she wants, she goes back into being an introvert. And becomes outraged with no compassion for anyone other than herself. And don't have any pity for the less unfortunate people in our society. She is a very disruptive person with her relationship with the men in her life and very generous to them with her emotions. It is as if she only cares about getting along with the male population, and the other human beings of this world don't mean any more to her than what she can get from them. She is a very good male attention grabber but fails to have the knowledge on how to keep their interest. And at the same time, she is estranged from other people in her life. She will have you thinking she doesn't have the men. Do you think she doesn't have the mental ability to comprehend or appreciate and distinguish the incentive to respect and understand other people's accomplishments objectively? And then she is left feeling jealous, hearted and envious of others. And then she turns back to the men in her life and becomes promiscuous with them, hoping to gain financial success for herself. But she finds that they have moved on, and they do not have any desire to be with her anymore or none of her quality time. And that makes her bitter, so now she starts with her deviousness and deceit to try and accomplish what she wants and needs. And comparing the quality to what she sees that everyone else has. And start to want what they have, so she sets out to get what they got or better. While still claiming she has done nothing in her past life that would have stopped or hindered her from being successful. The way she sees her failures is the fault of her parents, and now her culture has treated her. These roadblocks have prevented her from accomplishing her success earlier in life

Dorothy Mae Pickens Jenkins

Amplified Bible (Zondervan)

Proverbs: C8, V12

12) I' Wisdom [from God], make prudence in my dwelling, and I find knowledge and discretion [James 1:5].

Luke: C1, W7

77) To bring and give the knowledge of salvation to His people in the forgiveness and remission of their sins.

Psalm: C109, V2

2) For the mouths of the wicked and the mouth of deceit are opened against me: they have spoken to me and against me with lying tongues.

CHAPTER 2

RESPECT AND LOVE FOR ALL GENERATIONS

Common Sense

Mr. Navel has known this young man Willard all of his life, and he works so hard at two jobs. He works so hard that he and everyone around him knows he just works too much. And that he should take some time off to enjoy his family and the good things in life. What I'm trying to say is we may take it as being selfish on our part, but that's not our intent; we miss his presence. He is a remarkably caring human being, and when he's around, he brings loving, kindness, respect, and easy comprehension and communication with everyone around him. Leaving us with an opportunity to get to know him; if we allow ourselves, we can grasp on to a teachable moment.

But instead, a percent of us are looking at the structure of his face and body. Not giving any attention to his respecting spirit and not taking notice of his non-polluted language that's not coming from this man at all. Instead, we all are so busy checking him out. Until we have already allowed him to get to know us without even trying too. In all reality, we have already let him just touch him how to treat us without really trying, then later we asked ourselves, why doesn't he respect me. Because you touch him from the "beginning", he doesn't have "too", and he already feels like you don't deserve respect talking dating; if we as women don't have self-respect, we can't expect respect from dating, marriage or any relationship. We must know, we teach people how to treat us, just as I said before, if you show someone your don't care about being respected.

Then they will continue to disrespect you, whether it's man, woman, or just to get to know him before we start a relationship with him. Rather than putting so much emphasis on his facial and body structure. Let me appeal to you because we will know the way we are going to be treated by him in the months and years to come. It will mean more to us than the structure of his face and body. It's very hard to try and make someone respect you, then if you had demanded it from the beginning. And now we want him to respect us when this is all new to him because that isn't something he was doing in the beginning. Go back to when you first met him when he was a workaholic and still is. So how and why "is it '' you think the way he treats us is going to change if you allow him to treat you with disrespect from the beginning. Now you want to stop in the middle of the road and try to make him respect you. When he has not shown you any respect during the entire time he has known you, then we become angry because we are trying to make him do something he is not familiar with and has no knowledge of it at all. Because you did not show persistence or demand respect from the beginning. I'm not saying we will not get respect from him, but it's going to take some time with a lot of patience. Why is this happening? I will tell you why, because we never tried to get to know him or demand respect before we allow ourselves to start a relationship with him. Then she already had said to him, let's have a baby together; he says no and then we become very "angry" and say to yourself I'll get pregnant anyway. And thinking, oh am good enough to sleep with, but not suitable to have your baby? He said, no, he wasn't ready to have children, but we decided for him anyway when you made that decision to become a single mother. So don't blame him for not wanting to become a parent because of what you thought you wanted for yourself. You weren't ready to become a parent either; you only tried to get what you wanted for yourself as a woman. Trying to find a more permanent way to keep him with you and being so persistent in getting our way. We never thought about the endurance and obstacles we had to go through as women with our children. We then recognize we could have made better choices. Then if we are smart and have learned from our bad choices, we will come to a decision to know this is not as simple as saying he ruined my life. And start taking responsibility for your own life and stop blaming him and others for the way your life turns out. Stop and realize we are the ones in charge of our own life, not him.

Dorothy Mae Pickens Jenkins

Amplified Bible (Zondervan)

Psalm: C64, V9

9) And all men shall [reverently] fear and be in and they will declare the work of God, for they will wisely consider and knowledge that it is His doing.

Genesis: C2, V3

3) And God blessed (spoke good the seventh day, set it apart as His own, and hallowed it, because on it God rested from all His work which He had created and done. [Exod 20:11].

Psalm: C33, V4 & V8

4 For the word of the Lord is right and all His work Is done in faithfulness.

Let all the earth fear the Lord (reverse and worship Him] let all the inhabitants of the world stand in awe of Him.

Common Sense

Mr. Curtis said decent people, with esteem shows respect for other people especially to the elders, and giving consideration to all by expressing respect to all mothers and fathers. And Grandparents will express that same respect back to our children and all generations.

Dorothy Mae Pickens Jenkins

Amplified Bible (Zondervan)

Isaiah C30, V9

For this is a rebellious people, faithless and lying sons, children who will not hear the law and instruction of the Lord.

Ephesians C6, V3& V14 & V22

3) That it may be well with thee, and thou mayest live long on the earth

14) Stand therefore [hold your ground], having tightened the belt of truth around your loins and having put on the breastplate of integrity and of moral rectitude and right standing with God.

22) I have sent him to you for this very purpose, that you may know how we are and that he may console and cheer and encourage and strengthen your hearts.

Common Sense

Mrs Butch said we must have balance in our lives and we must treat each other with a valve of importance, with compassion in your heart. Keep balance in our life no matter the condition of our circumstances. Boundaries and balance will keep you in your proper perspective. So you will know you have enough sense to use our common sense, without getting out of balance, in our children, adults, and our aging elders. We have those qualities of keeping balance in our lives, it's like balancing the scales, only we call it the balancing act. But "honey" believe me it (ain't no act) is real.

Dorothy Mae Pickens Jenkins

Amplified Bible (Zondervan)

Proverbs: C11, VI
1 A false balance and up righteous dealings are extremely offensive and shamefully sinful to the Lord, but a just weight is His delight.

Proverbs: C16, V11
11) A just balance and scales are the Lord, all the weights of the bag are His work [established on His eternal principles].

Job: C31,V6
Oh, let me be weighed in a just balance and let Him weigh me, that God may know my integrity!

Hosea C12, V7
Canaan [Israel whose ideals have sunk to those of Canaan] is a trader: the balances of deceit are in his hand: he loves to oppress and defraud.

Common Sense

Nadia knew her cousin to be a very nice person with a caring heart; she was around her cousin from the day she was born. But they became friends later in life, as they grew up and became very close to each other. They were in each other's life when dating and holding down a full-time job, and raising her children. While Nadia's children were

27

all grown up and out of the house, she is a woman that has morals and always tries to be fair to everyone involved.

Whether it was relationships with a boyfriend, fiancee, or husband, she would not tolerate some things were hitting and being dishonest in a relationship, whether it was matters of the heart or kinfolk. Nadia had taken very good care of her children as they grew; she was a very hard working woman with a lot of discipline within herself. And teaching her children not to be insubordinate to her or to their authority figure. But she knew insubordinate people in her life that tried to control her, and she had the ability to not let men or anyone else control her. Nadia was very proud of her cousin, the way she handled people that tried to control her, especially the men in her life. She would step up and tell them that I will not be disrespected, then if they would not adapt to that, she had skills to show them. You will not disrespect me and send them on their way, and after some time had passed, they would regret it.And how did Nadia know this? Because she was fortunate enough to know the individual that she had sent him on his way, he came back and confided in her. This young woman is a very attractive, confident person. She is determined to accomplish anything she sets out to do. Where she had to tell you something, you don't want to hear, or you are just too ignorant to understand, or if you are plunging into complete denial.

Some would say she sounds like a Christian, but Nadia would say, yes, she goes to church quite often, maybe every Sunday. But that doesn't mean that a person like this young woman had to go to church to be a Christian. She had her good qualities within herself, before she attended the church house. She is someone to be admired, especially in our society today, and this young woman has been through some rough times. As Nadia has also, but she still remains a decent, compassionate person, packed with endurance. Nadia's view of this young woman, she is very proud to be a blood relative of hers. This vibrant young woman is now living in a town of about 325,000 people in a very nice house, nice neighborhood, with very nice neighbors. Continuing to be a very successful, productive, competitive, happy, desired human being with the righteousness of the heart, she is an asset to our family and society.

Dorothy Mae Pickens Jenkins

Amplified Bible (Zondervan)

Exodus C4, V12

12) Now therefore and I will be with your mouth and will teach you what you shall say.

Ephesians C4, V32

32) And become useful and helpful and kind to one another, tenderhearted (compassionate, understanding, loving-heart), forgiving one another [readily and freely], as God in Christ forgave you.

Psalm C30, V5

5) For His anger is but for a moment, but His favor is for a lifetime or in His favor is life. Weeping may endure for a night, but joy comes in the morning Cor 4:17].

Psalm C100, V5

5) For the Lord is good: His mercy and loving-kindness are everlasting. His faithfulness and truth endure to all generations.

Common Sense

Mrs. B said boundaries are important, and we must be generous by not allowing ourselves to push our ways on other people. And only thinking and accepting things the way we want them to be. All adults and children should know their limitations and stay within the boundaries of them. Boundaries are only giving respect to other individuals time to themselves, to have some freedom and control over their own lives. Be proud of yourself, and leave folk alone; allow them to be themselves. But keep in mind if you are married or have a significant other, know you must spend time with her or him. Do not become confused, and don't give yourselves the appropriate time that you need together. Have sense enough to know it is essential to your relationship that couples spend time with each other. If we don't, we are playing a dangerous game with each other. And you just might lose, listen to people; everyone has boundaries (it's called my space). I warn you when we are married, your space becomes our space. If you don't want to share your time with your husband, wife, or significant other, then we should not have gotten married. Don't push each other so far away because we might not make it back or can't get back to each other. Communication, respect and allowing respect to show up in you, is the key to love, staying in love, and making love. And yes, yes, when the romance and love making slow down, or if it is not even there anymore, you will still remain in love. Why? Because you respect each other and love comes from having respect for one another.

Dorothy Mae Pickens Jenkins

Amplified Bible (Zondervan)

Ephesians: C5, V2

2) And walk in love, [esteeming and delighting in one another] as Christ loved us and gave Himself up for us, a slain offering and sacrifice to God [for you, so that it became] a sweet fragrance [Ezek 20:41].

Colossians: C1, V10

10) That you may walk (live and conduct yourselves) in a manner worthy of the Lord, fully pleasing to Him and desiring to please Him in all things, bearing fruit in every good work and steadily growing and increasing in an by the knowledge of God [with fuller, deeper, and clearer.

Psalm: C143, V8

8) Know the way wherein I should walk, for I lift up my inner self to You.

Psalm: C111, V10

10) The reverent fear and worship of the Lord is the beginning of Wisdom and skill [the preceding and the first essential, the prerequisite and the alphabet]: a good understanding, wisdom, and meaning have all those who do [the will of the Lord] Their praise of Him endures forever [Job 28:28; Prov 1:7; Matt 22:37, 38: Rev 14:7].

Common Sense

Mrs. Joslyn said she met this attractive young woman named Susan, and it was something about her that everyone could see. She was very different from the average woman that Mrs. Joslyn had met before. Susan was not hostile or mean spirit; she had a very pleasant attitude about herself, making it very easy and comforting to be around. Mrs. Joslyn wasn't around her a lot, but when she was, she liked the way Susan treated her. It also made her like Susan more because she had drawn respect from her. And that made Mrs. Joslyn feel like she herself had met someone that had respect for herself and others. Something other women liked and acted like they didn't care about having respect for themselves and others. But Susan and her siblings sure did show respect for Mrs. Joslyn, which brought joy to Mrs. Joslyn heart.

Because that told her Susan cared about her and respected her. Mrs. Joslyn came to know they were the kind, nice people, she had even met in a long time. Susan was a very close friend to Mrs. Joslyn, and her entire family loved Mrs. Joslyn daddy. And that also made Mrs. Joslyn felt so very comfortable with Susan because she could see how much they loved her daddy. When she saw how they treated her daddy when she was around them, especially when they would stop by to see Mrs. Joslyn. Susan and her family would always talk about how good Mrs. Joslyn daddy was and how he was such a loving, caring man. And her daddy would always be welcome in their home. Mrs. Joslyn will never forget how Susan treated her; it made her joyful just to be around Susan and her family. Especially because she grew up around people that weren't nice at all by any means. And Susan, this respectful young lady is still in her life to this day, and Mrs. Joslyn has grown to love and respect her. Now Mrs. Joslyn has a grown daughter that reminds her of Susan, and her way of thinking is almost identical to Susan's philosophy of life. She is proud to have known such a young person of her caliber, that just let her know all young people are not disreputable people. So that leaves Mrs. Joslyn with a good feeling about our society that there is hope for our young people and her generation.

Dorothy Mae Pickens Jenkins

Amplified Bible (Zondervan)

Proverbs: C15, V33
33) The reverent and worshipful fear of the Lord brings instruction in Wisdom, and humility comes before honor.

Ephesians: C4, V2
2) Living as becomes you] with complete lowliness of mind (humility) and meekness (unselfishness, gentleness, mildness), with patience, bearing with one another and making allowances because you love one another.

James: C3, V13
13) Who is there among you who is wise and intelligent? Then let him by his noble living show forth his [good] works with the [unobtrusive] humility [which] is the proper attribute] of true wisdom.

James: C4, V10
10) Humble yourselves [feeling very insignificant] in the presence of the Lord, and He will exalt you [He will lift you up and make your lives significant].

Common Sense

Duncan, this man has issues when it comes to respecting his wife. He believes there is nothing wrong with him embracing and kissing other women in his wife's presence. He feels he should be able to act at his discretion, to how he interacts with other women. And the wife should adjust to it except it because that is part of his personality. Meanwhile, the wife is telling him it is very inappropriate behavior. And you are acting out of your own self-interest, and you know what you are doing is unjustifiable. And he lacks the ability to comprehend what she is saying to him. The inappropriate behavior of other women around your wife really bothers her and makes her extremely uncomfortably. He said it doesn't mean anything; it's just his way of saying hello. The wife said, it is unacceptable, you have to stop doing that, or you will not be able to live here in our home with me. He poised for a minute and said I think you are being very unfair, but I will stop, as you call it, the so call flirting. But now she realizes it just keeps happening, again and again; this is a total of about 7 years. The wife said again it should be a "priority" to you to use your intelligence, not nonsense. If you do not, I don't want you as my husband "anymore" do you understand? He said, yes, I understand I promise it will never happen again. It has not happened for 5 years, but too what the "relationship had to go through for the abuse to stop". Then the husband said to her after 5 years had passed, he did not think it was fair. Of her to be so persistent about how he acts with other women, and he thinks it was unfair. And he thinks he should be able to interact with other women according to the way he feels is appropriate to him, not her. So now he is disrespecting his wife by doing the same thing he was doing 5 years ago. Only now, he is doing it in public and in places when the wife is there or not there. Now the wife is just distraught; he indicates he is not interested in anything she is about to say. Or the least bit impressed at what she is about to say because she is only trying to make him feel like he is doing something wrong. So the wife can see that her husband is being extremely unfair or is he just amazingly arrogant or just ignorant. This is amazingly painful she's done, another marriage ruin, for lack of communication and understanding. When the adults

34

won't listen to each other, how are they going to be relentless in teaching their children how to communicate and respect each other?

Dorothy Mae Pickens Jenkins

Amplified Bible (Zondervan)

Genesis: C2, V24

24) Therefore a man shall leave his father and his mother and shall become united and cleave to his wife, and they shall become one flesh [Matt 19:5,1 Cor 6:16; Eph 5:31-33].

Ephesians: C5, V22, V23, & V33

Wives, be subject (be submissive and adapt yourselves) to your own husband's as [a service] to the Lord.

For the husband is head of the wife as Christ is the Head of the church Himself the savior of [His] body.

33) However, let each man of you [without exception] love his wife as [being in a sense] his very own self, and let the wife see that she respects and reverences her husband [that she notices him, regards him, honors him, prefers him, venerates, and esteems him: and that she defers to him, praises him, and loves and admires him exceedingly]. [1 Pet 3:2].

Common Sense

Mrs. Carter was the kind of lady who would say these words. Oh Father, I am so very proud to be your Daughter. I feel so grateful to be alive to show you that I have respect, kind feelings in my heart for everyone. It's like you have put me in my Mama's arms so I will be safe. Humble as I am, I need help to forgive people who have wronged me. Dear Father, I have never taken this long to forgive anyone before. I stand here asking you, dear God, help me to forgive those people, so I may go on living my life in peace. I am listening to you Father, because I know you are talking to me. But listen to me, Father, right now I can't hear you. Father, I know it's me not hearing you, just don't know what to do to help myself, help me, Father, I am your daughter. It's in your word that you do not lie. So I am asking in your Son's name help me so that my heart can stop hurting.

Dorothy Mae Pickens Jenkins

Amplified Bible (Zondervan)

II Chronicles: C33, V12

12) And when he was in affection, he besought the Lord his God and humbled himself greatly before the God of his Fathers.

Number: C12, V3

3) Now the man Moses was very meek gentle, kind, and humble, or above all the men on the face of the earth.

II Chronicles: C34, V27

27) Because your heart was tender and penitent and humbled yourself before God when you heard His words against this place and its inhabitants, and humbled yourself before Me and rent your clothes and wept before Me. I have heard you, says the Lord.

Daniel: C2, V20

20) Daniel answered, Blessed be the name of God forever and ever! For wisdom and might are His!

Common Sense

Mrs. Britt said self-discipline is important; the discipline she is speaking of is keeping control of one's mind and emotions. Do not allow yourself to be involved with people that make us feel they have more control over yourself than we do. If you feel threatened around them, remove yourself from the unpleasantness. Try to avoid being around people that make you uncomfortable, but we know that is not always possible. So we must understand, it is your responsibility to be in control of our emotions. As we mature, our feelings change, that is why I am assuring you, if we use our common sense. We will be able to control those different feelings as we mature. Your mannerism will become different, and there will be some eager desires, feeling anxious that' s normal. And at the same time, you have to trust what you are feeling. And learn to cope, and sort out who you are and what you are feeling. It helps us to stay in control in the adult world. and society. As adults, let us keep the proper perspective of self-discipline in our lives.

Dorothy Mae Pickens Jenkins

Amplified Bible (Zondervan)

2 Timothy: C1, V7

7) For God did not give us the spirit of timidity (of cowardice, of craven and cringing and fawning fear), but [He has given us a spirit] of power and of love and of calm and well-balanced mind and discipline and self-control.

II Peter: C1, V6 & V7

And in [exercising] knowledge [develop] self-control [develop] steadfastness (patience, endurance), and in [exercising) steadfastness [develop] godliness (piety).

And in [exercising] godliness [develop] brotherly affection, and in [exercising] brotherly affection [develop] Christian Love.

II Peter: C1, V5

5) For this very reason, adding your diligence [to the divine promise], employ every effort in exercising your faith to develop virtue (excellence, resolution, Christian energy) and in [exercising] virtue [develop] knowledge (intelligence).

Common Sense

Mrs. Mars said, don't allow your significant other to not hold you in a worthy place in his life of importance. Once you allow someone to place you secondary to someone else, that is a sign of disrespect. And if you don't say or do anything about it, they will do it again. And when it is done to you again, he will look for her to accept it; she will find herself not wanting to accept this way of treatment. Because it makes her very uncomfortable and her heart is hurting, she then looks back to when she first started dating him. What exactly did she' allow him to say or do to her that was unacceptable to the relationship. Now she looks back and remembers what he said which was that he was not really dating her exclusively. How can she be upset with him because she now sees another person in their relationship other than the two of them? Because he told her that without saying the word exclusively, his actions told her they were exclusive. But now she is all hurt and feeling some kind way. The trouble with some of us is that we don't pay attention to what is not being said. We need to take notes on what is being said and how he said it. What should be understood is there should not be any other woman in his life that he put before her. If you have allowed it once and there were no consequences to him, he is not going to make any effect of changing. Unless she said to him, it is simply not acceptable, but keep in mind it may be too late to make a change as far as he is concerned. So now she has got an issue between the two of them, and a difficult decision will have to be made. He really doesn't care about making decisions because he knows exactly what he's going to do for himself, and she is not included. It's all about self preference this time around with him. Then she starts to feel sorry for herself and allows herself to become depressed. She knows how this is affecting her but keeps lying to herself and pushing herself to the effect where she starts to blame others for her position. And none of this is her fault, but she knows probably most of it is her fault. Because she was not listening and taking notes on what was being said and not said.

What she needed to learn is take responsibility for her own life and not leave it to someone else. And then blame them for something she neglected to do for her own self. Now she is angry because she realized he only wanted to have a one-sided relationship and be pleasing to himself only. And there is no room for anyone else, and he will never be able to give her what she wants or needs. Because he will say she is too needy and her necessities overwhelmed him. What ever happened to her? She went away and never came bad.

Dorothy Mae Pickens Jenkins

Amplified Bible (Zondervan)

Psalm: C37, V39
39) But the salvation of the [consistently] righteous is the Lord: He is

their Refuse and secure Stronghold in the time of trouble.

Matthew C26, V22 & V41

22) They were exceedingly pained and distressed and deeply hurt and sorrowful and began to say to Him one after another. "Surely it cannot be I, Lord, can.

41) All of you must keep awake (give strict attention, be cautious and active) and watch and pray, that you may not come into temptation . The spirit indeed is willing, but the flesh is weak.

CHAPTER 3

THE QUALITY OF BEING HONEST

Common Sense

Mrs. Mookie said there are many different types of people in our society that will try and control our lives. They are so caught up in their own way of thinking and doing things, they are arrogant, conceited, selfish, and self-conscious people. They are so controlling it doesn't matter to them whether they're wrong or not. As long as they can make you feel powerless and beneath them, it allows them to feel better about themselves. Because the most important thing to them is making you feel bad about yourself. In all honesty how could a person like that live with all of that deceit. Because those kinds of people don't have a conscience, in fact their only interest is self-interest and power.

Dorothy Mae Pickens Jenkins

Amplified Bible (Zondervan)

Thessalonians: C4, V4
4) That each of you should know how to possess (control, manage) his own body in consecration (purity, separated from things profane) and honor.

James: C3, V2
2) For we all often stumble and fall and offend in many things. Anyone does not offend in speech [never says the wrong things], he is fully

developed character and a perfect man, able to control his whole body and to curb his entire nature.

II Corinthians: C5, V14

14) For the love of Christ controls and urges and impels us, because we are of the opinion and conviction that [if] One died for all, then all died:

James: C3, V8

8) But the human tongue can be tamed by no man It is restless (undisciplined, irreconcilable) evil, full of deadly poison.

Common Sense

Carly is the kind of person who doesn't care about what you said or cares less about what is right or wrong. She knows what is right but chose to do nothing about doing right. She cares less about what is essential to love, life and people. Her pleasures are her goals, and she has no common senses or concerns. Because she has nothing to offer anyone, and certainly not for the common good of our society.

Dorothy Mae Pickens Jenkins

Amplified Bible (Zondervan)

Philippians: C4, V5

5) Let all men know and perceive and recognize your unselfishness (your considerateness, your forbearing spirit). The Lord is near [He is coming soon].

Exodus: C23, V21

21) Give heed to him, listen to and obey His, voice be not rebellious

before Him or provoke Him, for He will not pardon your transgression, for My Name is in Him.

Galatians: C6, V18
18) The grace (spiritual favor, blessing) of our Lord Jesus Christ (the Anointed One, the Messiah) be with your spirit, brethren. Amen (so be it).

Ephesians: C3, V2
2) Assuming that you have heard of the stewardship of God's grace (His unmerited favor) that was entrusted to me [to dispense to you] for your benefit.

Common Sense

This is Lottie story; what is absolutely amazing to me is this lady didn't care about "anything" or "anyone" other than "herself". This woman lived in an apartment, and as you walk through the door, you could see the bugs crawling. Annie asked her would she like for her to help get rid of them. She said no because there will come a time that she and her children will have to eat those bugs. Sometimes, a month passed, and she and her children didn't have anything left in the house but those bugs. And if she had to eat them to keep from going hungry, they would do so. Don't you never try to kill any of these bugs in my house? It seems she got very angry with Annie concerning the bugs problems and Annie didn't understand why she didn't work or go to school. And Mrs. Annie never saw her do anything but be with men. And allowed men to stay with her and her children, Mrs. Annie didn't like it or understand. So Mrs. Annie wouldn't go around her too much anymore.

Mrs Annie felt very uncomfortable around her and her family. Mrs. Annie especially didn't like her so-called man, it seemed to her he only worked sometimes, and they just lay around the apartment. Lottie and her man didn't have any goals or ambition for themselves or the children for the future. It seems they were very much into each other sexually, but it seems Lottie was more into seducing him. Her total tantalization was to trap him into having sex with her and not being able to turn away from her. She didn't care about what he wanted; it was always about what she wanted and when. It is fundamentally essentially, unconditionally, positively and completely her way with him knowing he had better comprehend every bite of what she wanted from him It was as if she was an envelope to him, and he made all of his personal deposit there. And the children somehow didn't matter because as long as she could keep him, nothing else mattered much. As keeping him consumed with the lightness of her, she felt that he would not ever leave her Lottie thought she was the prettiest, the most beautiful shaped woman she or anyone had ever seen in their entire life. And he could not "leave" her, even if he wanted too. But he did leave her even though he himself thought he could not.

Dorothy Mae Pickens Jenkins

Amplified Bible (Zondervan)

Ephesians: C4, V18

18) Their moral understanding is darkened and their reasoning is beclouded [They are] alienated (estranged, self-banished) from the life of God [with no share in it: this because of ignorance (the want of knowledge and perception, the willful blindness) that is deep-seated in them, due to their hardness of heart [to the insensitiveness of their moral nature.

Titus: C1, V13

13) And this account of them is [really] true Because it is [true], rebuke them sharply [deal sternly, even severely with them], so that they may be sound in the faith and free from error.

II Peter: C1, V6

6) And in [exercising] knowledge [develop] self-control, and in [exercising] self control [develop] steadfastness (patience, endurance), and in [exercising] steadfastness [develop] godliness (piety).

II Peter: C2, V3

3) And in their covetousness (lust, greed) they will exploit you with false (cunning) arguments. From of old the sentence [of condemnation] for them has not been idle: their destruction (eternal misery) has not been asleep.

Common Sense

Ruby is a conversationalist, and she said the importance of having a conversation is to keep the respect of showing integrity. Whether you think what you have to say is much more important than others or not. Because isn't that what a conversation is? Having common sense enough to know there are other people would like to contribute to the conversation also. But the conversationalist is so busy trying to keep the attention on herself she forgets about everyone else and pushes them out. Now she is left feeling arrogant, foolish, pitiful, and filled with embarrassment. So what she knows now is she has abused the conversation. And if she had allowed someone else to talk maybe, she could have learned something. Now she never learned anything or contributed to the conversation. The conversationalist is left feeling empty and remorseful, but will they admit it? Of course not; they would rather go through the same thing again, at another time.

Dorothy Mae Pickens Jenkins

Amplified Bible (Zondervan) Job:

C13, V6, V7, & V8

Hear now my reasoning, and listen to the pleadings of my lips.

Will you speak unrighteously for God and talk deceitfully for Him?

Will you show partiality to Him [be unjust to me in order to gain favor with Him]? Will you act as special pleaders for God?

Corinthians C4, V20

20) For the kingdom of God consists of and is based on not talk but power (moral power and excellence of soul).

Common Sense

Jocelyn is the kind of person that comes to you with good warm overflowing "hospitable behavior"; it only lasts for a little while. Because the "leash" she is, has to come out, making themselves feel better that they made a fool of you and others. The generosity they show you, in the beginning, is a coerce, so they may worm their backside into our lives. And stay in our lives by any means necessary. Remember, there is always a big payoff for them, and numerous ways always remind us they don't need anyone to vouch for them. They give a lot of loyalty to you by allowing you to know how good they have been to you, "family",, friends and others. In reality, they don't like being so hospitable, but that is what makes them try and keep you thinking they are kind-hearted. And they keep that feeling of being a great person with generosity for the rest of their deceitful life, and it becomes their lifestyle. And very patiently waiting on their "next potential victim". These people are like an "athlete"; they "practice" to become good at what they do. Because they are always at practice every day and everyone is a potential victim. In the end, he or she feels like a victim because they themselves have violated so many people. But she is not a victim; she is just out in society with all the other mix minded, deceitful people like herself.

Dorothy Mae Pickens Jenkins

Amplified Bible (Zondervan)

Proverbs: C22, V10
10) Drive out the scoffer, and contention will go out: yes, strife and abuse will cease.

Proverbs: C19, V25
25) Strike a scoffer, and the simple will learn prudence: reprove a man of understanding and he will increase in knowledge.

Proverbs: C14, V17
17) He who foams up quickly and flies into a passion deals foolishly, and a man of wicked plots and plans is hated.

Romans: C6, V12
12) Let not sin therefore rule as king in your mortal (short-lived, perishable) bodies, to make you yield to its cravings and be subject to its lusts and evil passions.

47

Common Sense

Nicole said favor is given to us; if we allow ourselves to be kind to each other, we are allowing favor to work through our hearts. Some of us chose not to use it, so therefore we become a disappointment to society, ourselves and the people around us. Our suggestibility is harshness with ridicule toward others to make yourself feel better. Your brain has become a disease, so, therefore, we have nothing to think about; we are so self-absorbed, we don't have grace. But if somehow we become aware that we have grace by then we are so self-righteous we wouldn't allow ourselves to use it. Recognizing grace is wonderful, and we should pass it down to our children, grandchildren, and all generations around us.

Dorothy Mae Pickens Jenkins

Amplified Bible (Zondervan)

1 Corinthians: C15, V10

10) But by the grace (the unmerited favor and blessing) of God I am what I and his grace toward me was not [found to be] for nothing (fruitless and without effect) In fact, I worked harder than all of them [the apostles], though it was not really but grace (the unmerited favor and blessing) of God which was with me.

Job: C10, V3 & V12

3) Does it seem good to You that You should oppress, that You should despite and reject the work of Your hands, and favor the schemes of the wicked?

12) You have granted me life and favor, and Your providence has preserved my spirit.

Ephesians: C1, V7

7) In Him we have redemption (deliverance and salvation) through His blood, the remission (forgiveness) of our offenses (shortcomings and trespasses), in accordance with the riches and the generosity of His gracious favor.

Common Sense

Grandma Waters said outsiders tend to mislead by making a fool of you and yours. And may bring harm to the family, and they are flaky people. Don't be so easy to believe what people tell you because we know in our hearts of hearts what's right and what is wrong. We must have the right standards within ourselves to make the right decision for all concern. Outsiders could be misleading people and lead you into the wrong way of life by convincing you their life is a better way of living. But you know what is necessary to keep yourself from being swayed their way.

Although the outsider could be the stranger that's living in your home, and you could be subdued by the hands of a stranger. But we find it wasn't an outsider, after all, who brought physical harm to the home; it was already there. Sometimes it's right there in the home with us, and we don't know it. I think grandma Waters knew the stranger was in the house but chose to say nothing.

Because she believes in her heart that a family member would have killed him if she had acknowledged it. Then what does the family do in this house? They act kindly toward each other and pretend nothing has happened or changed. As an adult, she found that some of the relatives did not want to associate with her because they thought she was like a stranger in the house. But the truth is she is nothing like the stranger; she is the victim just as the others were. She had to focus on herself and her children to make sure the stranger didn't bring harm to her children. It was very clear to her; she would bring physical harm to anyone that tried to hurt her or her children and would not think twice about it. So you see, the stranger doesn't have to be an outsider; he could be the stranger right in your own home. Talk to your children, love and protect them with all that we have. Use our everlasting perseverance means "steadfastness", don't ever let anyone take your dignity away from you.

Dorothy Mae Pickens Jenkins

Amplified Bible (Zondervan)

Psalm: C5, V4 & V6

4) For You are not a God Who takes pleasure in wickedness, neither will evil [man] so much as dwell [temporarily] with You.

6) You will destroy those who speak lies; the Lord abhors [and rejects] the bloodthirsty and deceitful man.

Proverbs: C2, V22 & V13

22) But the wicked shall be cut off from the earth, and the treacherous shall be rooted out of it.

13) Men who forsake the paths of the uprightness to walk in the ways of darkness.

Common Sense

Mrs. Gina said we don't have to be a volatile person or use violence's to kill someone; we can kill them with words. Some people are not capable of being attainable to have any ability or quality to care about

50

other people. Somewhere in their sick little mind, they think, for some reason, others are willing to affectingly kiss their butts until death. And they should have all the ingredients in them for kissing their butts because they don't think any more of you. Then they did of the dog that they step on while walking, and immediately she can destroy his self-worth. They feel like you are no more than a pea brain to them anyway. And you don't do as they want you too, when they want you too, and how they want too, you become no use to them. And even after you are dead, they still treat you like you are an unwanted dead dog. Once you are gone, they have no sympathy toward how you look lying there in the casket, ready to be buried. And didn't carry out any of your wishes, but when they first met you, they immediately turned on their charming affection and attached themselves to you like a magnet to a refrigerator door.

Dorothy Mae Pickens Jenkins

Amplified Bible (Zondervan)

Proverbs: C28, V26

He who leans on, trust in, and is confident of his own mind and heart is a [self-confident] fool, but he who walks in skillful and godly Wisdom shall be delivered [James 1:5].

Deuteronomy: C8, V5

Know also in your [minds and] hearts that, as a man disciplines and instructs his son, so the Lord your God disciplines and instructs you.

Deuteronomy: C8, V6

So you shall keep the commandments of the Lord your God, to walk in His ways and [reverently] fear Him [Prov 8:13].

Proverbs: C8, V13

The reverent fear and worshipful awe of the Lord [includes] the hatred of evil; pride, arrogance, the evil way, and perverted and twisted speech I hate.

Common Sense

Nancy has no integrity; she is a person that made a conscious decision to deceive someone. With a deceiving personality to be self-seeking to whatever she wants for herself. A person has no sense of ethics or boundaries; these people feel hyper when they pull off something deceitful. Especially when they succeed in getting what they want out of it. They get satisfaction out of thinking that we were stupid or naive enough to have to trust them. They come off as very pleasant, kind and caring people at first, but they are the complete opposite inside. And we are looking at them with elementary psychology because we think that's all that we needed for this person. Because of all the kindness they have shown us, it would be just what it calls for, which is an elementary decision on our behalf. But they knew from the beginning, they were out for self-seeking ideas for their own gain. Somewhere in their malice little mind, it might bring them some sort of respect while deceiving them. There is no behavior in their pompous life that they know about any importance in being a decent person. The fact is that you are of no significance or value to yourself or our society and surely not our principles. These people have no moral compass; they are strictly thinking and operating in their own best interest in acquiring whatever they want. They have impurities in their heart that no one can get rid of. As mama grand once said, if you keep company with someone that doesn't have a pure heart, you had better mind your company. Because sometimes they are only out to manipulate you into their way of thinking and acting. Once they start their infectious ideas on you, there is a tendency to lean toward their behavior. If you start to see that happening, we need to pull away from that person because they don't mean you any earthly "Good". A self seeker is not a person that we want to build a relationship with.

Dorothy Mae Pickens Jenkins

Amplified Bible (Zondervan)

Proverbs: C11, V20
20) They who are willfully contrary in heart are extremely disgusting and shamefully vile in the eyes of the Lord, but such as are blameless and wholehearted in their ways are His delight!

Proverbs: C24, V28
28) Be not a witness against your neighbor without cause, and deceive not with your lips.

Matthew: C24, V4
4) Jesus answered them Be careful that no one misleads you [deceiving you and leading you into error].

Matthew: C11, V14
14) And if you are willing to receive and accept it John himself is Elijah who was to come [before the kingdom]. [Mal 4:51].

CHAPTER 4

RIGHTEOUSNESS AND RESPONSIBILITIES

Common Sense

Mr Henry said somewhere in all of our lives, we were taught responsibility. We all know what responsibility is, being accountable for what we are supposed to do. Being able to think for yourself and do what is right. Acting with reasonable ability to become trustworthy and reliable. Feeling an obligation toward your families, relatives, friends and society.

Dorothy Mae Pickens Jenkins

Amplified Bible (Zondervan)

Ruth C4, V16

16) And Naomi took the child, and laid it in her bosom and became a nurse unto it.

Ephesians C4, V24

24) And that ye put on the new man, which after God is created in righteousness and true holiness.

Proverbs C31, V26

26) She opens her mouth in skillful and godly Wisdom, and on her tongue is the law of kindness [giving counsel and instruction] Proverbs C1, V7.

7) The revenant and worshipful fear of the Lord is the beginning and the principal and choice part of knowledge [its starting point and its essence]: but fools despise skillful and godly Wisdom, instruction, and discipline [Ps 111:10].

Common Sense

Mr. PJ said some of us like to blame others for our shortcomings. But if we would use our common sense, we would have not, and will not, need a scapegoat for our life. Because we would not be making some of the same simple stupid mistakes. Then we turn right around and try to blame someone for our mistakes. Stop being so reckless and hot-tempered with your life and admit your mistakes. Grow better, start taking responsibility for the life we have been given.

Dorothy Mae Pickens Jenkins

Amplified Bible (Zondervan)

II Corinthians C8, V20

20) For we are our guard, intending that no one should fine anything for which to blame us in regard to our administration of this large contribution.

II Corinthians: C6, V3

3) We put on obstruction in anybody's way we give no offense in anything, so that no fault may Be found and our ministry blamed and discredited.

Genesis: C43, V9

9) I will be security for him: you shall require him of me [personally]: if I do not bring him back to you and put him before you, then let me

bear the blame forever.

Genesis: C44, V32

32) For your servant because security for the lad to my father, saying If I do not bring it to you, then I will bear the blame to my father forever.

Common Sense

Mr. Bucket said working is the first necessity of the house rules and principles. We start teaching our children around two or three years old, simple things they must do around the house and in their rooms. The first job the children had was picking the paper up from the floors and emptying the trash cans. As the children matured, they learned to cook, clean their rooms, and later the whole house. If you were a man child, you would take out the trash and cut the grass. We as parents have to teach our children a sense of responsibility and purpose in life, and the first necessity is you must work It is as simple as knowing we must have a roof over our head's food to eat, clothes on our backs and shoes on our feet. And water and soap to wash our bodies and clothes.

Dorothy Mae Pickens Jenkins

Amplified Bible (Zondervan)

Psalm: C104, V23

23) Man goeth forth unto his work and to his labor until the evening.

Proverbs: C24, V27

27) Put first things first Prepare your work outside and get it ready for yourself in the field, and afterward build your house and establish a home.

Titus: C3, V1

1) REMIND PEOPLE to be submissive to [their] magistrates and authorities, to be obedient, to be prepared and willing to do any upright and honorable work.

Deuteronomy C15, V10

10) You shall give to him freely without begrudging it: because of this the Lord will bless you in all your work and in all you undertake.

Common Sense

Aunt Victoria said there are not too many people in this world she has met who are like these women. She has learned so much from them they have taken time out of their busy lives to teach her. Some fears, values that she seriously needed, and wanted them to know she never considered she was wasting her time with them. To her, it was essential not to neglect their duties to the younger women and teach the young women about the responsibilities of life.

Living by the word of truth and with the wisdom of the older women. Therefore, help her accomplish all the requirements; Aunt Victoria needed to live to sustain all of her circumstances. Some had professional jobs, and others did not, but they all had maintained successful lives. And they are very satisfied with the way they live today and are highly respected by everyone who crosses their paths. If we can get wisdom from our elders and associate with them long enough to relate to them, we can hand this down to the even younger women. Then we are helping to give back by not giving up on our babies; let's enhance them by giving them our wisdom. And the righteousness of the word and the responsibilities of sharing it. A lot of us were raised by old school parents, and we already had some wisdom within us, which made some of us easy to deal with. And we had a better understandingof what our old school parents were teaching us. Just as these ladies were more sensitive to our needs by responding to the needs of our situations. By surrounding us with their love and the love of righteousness and kindness. These ladies are full of grace, integrity, respect, understanding, compassion, and an obligation of communication to themselves and others. As I said before, some of the women did not have professional jobs, but they still became good productive human beings in our society. And were able to help many other people learn how we should treat each other no matter the culture or religion. In regard to society, some of the women worked as domestic workers, stay at home moms, and single mothers. And what is so startling to some of our society they think women like these are not capable of earning a successful life for themselves. And some people will not lift a hand to help these women even if they could. But what they do is sit back and belittle this part of our society or show signs of a dislike for them. And in feeling this way, they "resent" them because they had or have successful careers. And they feel resentful toward them because they attended college to get their success. They feel that if you didn't go to college, you don't "deserve" to live and enjoy the same lifestyle as they. People like these women have a quality of self-worth within them, educated or not. If we communicate to each other and come to a whole as a communicator within our society. We will close that gap between us from being discriminating toward each other, and then maybe we can see our way to help each other. It is a necessity that we abolish this type of attitude and treatment of women who are less fortunate.

It's going to take a lot of grace and elegance to get rid of this type of behavior by making a commitment to each other. And stop engaging in digging ditches for others in our society, and things will change for the better for everyone concerned. We have to specifically connect and understand each other by staying away from denial and be acceptable to all different people. And we will become a beautiful society, full of excellence and righteousness in everything we do.

Dorothy Mae Pickens Jenkins

Amplified Bible (Zondervan)

Galatians: C6, V6

6) Let him who receives instruction in the Word [of God] share all good things with his teacher [contributing to his support].

Galatians: C5, V26

26) Let us not become vainglorious and self-conceited, competitive and challenging and provoking and irritating to one another, envying and being jealous of one another.

Proverbs: C14, V8

8) The Wisdom [godly Wisdom, which is a comprehensive insight [into the ways and purposes of God] of the prudent is to understand his way, but the folly of [self-confident] fools is to deceive.

Proverbs: C15 & V21

21) Folly is pleasure to him who is without heart and sense, but a man of understanding walks uprightly [making straight his course] 5:15].

Common Sense

Mrs. Asbury said, let the children talk, and as adults, we should allow ourselves to listen to them. We should want to listen to our children with our heart open and allow ourselves to know how they are feeling. I would like for them to listen to us so we can listen and learn from their generation. Let the children tell us what they want from us, tell us what they want us to do for them. We will listen, and we will hear them. Anything our children want to you say to us, we want to hear it, and we will hear you. Let us use our ability by allowing our common sense to take pleasure in listening and helping them. And as adults, we may help ourselves also, so you and I can learn from each other. We will do whatever it takes to open our hearts up to each other. We have to do this because our hearts need to be truthful with each other. We need you and your generation's advice, and the truth is we are nothing without the love and trust of our children. Don't fear us because there is favor over your generation and all generations to come. We are concerned about the way our society is today, just as you are. Our adult generation knows it is a necessity that we reach each other and help ourselves, stop looking for someone else to do it for us. If we do not come together in love, our generations will not have a successful future. We were born to be successful, passionate people; there is no way we can fail if we give our best.

Dorothy Mae Pickens Jenkins

Amplified Bible (Zondervan)

Deuteronomy C6, V7

7) You shall whet and sharpen them so as to make them penetrate, and teach and impress them diligently upon the [mind and] hearts of your children, and shall talk of them when you walk by the way, and when you lie down and when you rise up.

Jeremiah C50, V4

4) In those days and at time, says the Lord, the children of Israel shall come, they and the children of Judah together, they shall come up weeping as they come and seek the Lord their God [inquiring for and of Him and requiring Him, both by right of necessity and of the promises of God's Word].

Proverbs C22, V15

15) Foolishness is bound up in the heart of a child but the rod of discipline will drive it far from him.

1 Corinthians C3, V19

19) For this world's wisdom is foolishness (absurdity and stupidity) with God, for it is written He lays hold of wise in their [own] craftiness: [Job 5:13].

Common Sense

Mr Coleman said when the word woe is used, we must be consistent in our belief. And have confidence in one's abilities to do what is necessary. Be very sure your mind is not confused, and you are functioning from a firm foundation. Because we know when the word woe is used, poverty is right there with us. And where poverty is, I promise you, there will be some dysfunctional things going on in the family. But there is no excuse for our generation of children or the next generation not to grow up and live successful lives. The good has to be in your heart, mind and soul.

Dorothy Mae Pickens Jenkins

Amplified Bible (Zondervan)

Psalm: C34, V17

17) When the righteous cry for help, the Lord hears, and delivers them out of all their distress and troubles.

Psalm: C9, V9

9) The Lord also will be a refuge and a high tower for the oppressed, a refuge and a stronghold in times of trouble (high cost, destitution, and desperation).

1 Corinthians: C16, V13

13) be alert and on your guard: stand firm in your faith (your conviction respecting man's relationship to God and divine things, keeping the trust and holy fervor born of faith and a part of it). Act like men and be courageous, grow in strength! [Ps 31:24].

James: C1, V5

5) If any of you is deficient in wisdom, let him ask of the living God gives] to everyone liberally and ungrudgingly, without reproaching or faultfinding, and it will be given him.

Common Sense

Mr. Alvin James said we can't have a soul without a mind; good or bad, the mind is there. It just depends on you to have a desire to do good wills and purpose. Be careful not to subject your conceited mind to harm others. The intelligence of the mind is very easy to read, especially if you are determined to try and hide the ability to digest what you want to say or keep to yourself and can't. The mind develops your intellect; it is totally different from what your real conversation is. With your purpose and intellect showing us just who and what you are.

Dorothy Mae Pickens Jenkins

Amplified Bible (Zondervan)

Luke: C2, V35

35) And a sword will pierce through your own soul and also that the secret thoughts and purposes of many hearts may be brought out and disclosed.

Luke: C12, V20

20) But God said to him, You fool! This very night, they [the messengers of God,] will demand your soul for you, and all the things that you have prepared, whose will they be?

Job: C33, V17

17) That He may withdraw man from his purpose and cut off pride from him [disgusting him with his own disappointing self-sufficiency].

Proverbs: C12, V5

5) The thoughts and purposes of the [consistently] righteous are honest and reliable, but the counsels and designs of the wicked are treacherous.

Common Sense

Dan is a self-righteous thirty-five-year-old man; he must stop being a slave to his own self righteous ideals. He feels he is the only one who can give good advice, but he is not the only one who can. We can't lie within our conversations and figure we can teach our children right from wrong. Our children are intelligent enough to know when we are being deceitful, so know it is essential, to be honest and loyal in loving them with unconditional love.

Dorothy Mae Pickens Jenkins

Amplified Bible (Zondervan)

Galatians: C5, V26

26) Let us not become vainglorious and self-conceited, competitive and challenging and provoking and irritating to one another, envying and being jealous of one another.

1-Peter: C2, V15

15) For it is God's will and intention that by doing right [your good and honest lives] should silence (muzzle, ignorant charges and ill-informed criticisms of foolish person.

Galatians: C6, V4 & V5

let every person carefully scrutinize and examine and test his own conduct and his own work. He can then have the personal satisfaction and joy of doing something commendable [in itself alone] without [resorting boastful comparison with his neighbor.

Common Sense

Mr. Tippy said, "If we are insecure about ourselves, how is it that we think we are going to raise our children up to be secure, sensitive, responsible, and respectful human beings." We must stop doing our personal pleasure and allow our work to take all of our time and spend more time with our children. How can you say I love you and never be consistent with our quality time with them? We must leave our children with pleasant memories, not OPP (our personal pleasures). As parents, it is our responsibility to support and supply their needs and some of their wants. Please don't suppress our children with neglect; that will drive them to rebellion Falling straight into a stranger's arms and their lifestyle. This will happen because we are so insecure in ourselves; we are afraid of being firm and dedicated. To make sure they grow up to be well rounded, responsible, good human being. Our children need structure in their life, and that's starts at home with the love and responsibility of good parenting skills. We want our children to grow up into good ethical educated normal adults, not falling down into the dirt. And lying in it until it becomes mud, and they continue to sit in it. They must have enough self-worth to constantly start all over again no matter what. If we want to raise average and extraordinary children, we had better stop "procrastinate" and stop allowing our children to "negotiate" with us on how we should "raise them". For the sake of all parents and society, we will only bring harm, insecurities, confusion, and misguided children to our communities for generations.Surely our children, grandchildren, great-grandchildren and great-greatgrandchildren deserve better than that.

Dorothy Mae Pickens Jenkins

Amplified Bible (Zondervan)

Proverbs: C31, V26
She opens her mouth in skillful and godly Wisdom, and on her tongue is the law of kindness [giving counsel and instruction].

Proverbs: C31, V27
She looks well to how things go in her household, and the bread of idleness (gossip, discontent, and self-pity) she will not eatTim 5:14: Tit 2:5].

Exodus: C20, V6

But showing mercy and steadfast love to a thousand generations of those who love Me and keep My commandments.

Exodus: C20, V12

Regard (treat with honor, due obedience, and courtesy) your father and mother, that your days may be long in the land the Lord your God gives you.

CHAPTER 5

KNOWLEDGE AND WISDOM

Common Sense

Mr. Tricky said knowledge is obtainable; we must have enough self-confidence and know that common sense is one of the necessary tools that we have been given. Accept the gift that's given you, and be thankful for it. Use your common sense and education together, and I assure you, we will have a successful life with knowledge and prosperity.

Dorothy Mae Pickens Jenkins

Amplified Bible (Zondervan)

I Corinthians: C1, V4

4) I thank my God at all times for you because of the grace (the favor and spiritual blessing) of God which was bestowed on you in Christ Jesus.

Proverbs: C14, V6

6) A scoffer seeks Wisdom in vain [for his very attitude blinds and deafens him to it], but knowledge is easy to him who [feeling teachable] understands.

Proverbs: C2, V10

10) When wisdom entereth into thine heart, and knowledge is pleasant

unto thy soul.

Proverbs: C3, V13

13) Happy is the man that findeth wisdom, and the man that getteth understanding.

Common Sense

Mr Lee said, 'Information is the obtaining of knowledge and facts. The more knowledge you have, the more potential success will come through our accomplishments we make in life".

Dorothy Mae Pickens Jenkins

Amplified Bible (Zondervan)

Proverbs: C23, V26

26) My son gave me thine heart, and let thine eyes observe my ways.

Proverbs: C14, V6

6) A scoffer seeks Wisdom in vain [for his very attitude blinds and deafens him to it]. but knowledge is easy to him who [being teachable] understands.

Proverbs: C19, V2

Desire without knowledge is not good, and to be overhasty is to sin and miss the mark.

Proverbs: C30, V3

I have not learned skillful and godly Wisdom, that I should have the knowledge or burden of the Holy One.

Common Sense

Ray needs recognition to recognize who he is; he must be able to like himself and lose that sense of entitlement. Because when we have a sense of entitlement, it stops us from maturing and accepting the reality of the real world. It's impossible to do if you choose not to recognize who you are and have confidence in one's self-worth. To feel capable of caring about other people more than you care about yourself and your self-righteous ideas. It is impossible to do if you choose not to recognize who you are. Have confidence in oneself to feel capable of caring about other people more than your own self-righteous ideals.

Dorothy Mae Pickens Jenkins

Amplified Bible (Zondervan)

Galatians: C5, V23

23) Gentleness, meekness, humility, self-control, self-restraint, continence Against such things there is no law that can bring a charge.

Proverbs: C14, V26

26) In the reverent and worshipful fear of the Lord there is strong confidence, and His children shall always have a place of refuge.

John: C16, V33

33) I have told you these things, so that in Me you may have [perfect] peace and confidence In the world you have tribulation and trials and distress and frustration, but be of good cheer [take courage, be confident, certain, undaunted]! For 1 have overcome the world have deprived it of power to harm you and have conquered it for you].

Titus: C3, V2

yielding, gentle, and conciliatory and to show unqualified courtesy toward everybody.

Common Sense

Mrs English said we must understand, and comprehend what someone is saying to us. And be able to understand what we are reading, hearing, and having the ability to learn from it.

Dorothy Mae Pickens Jenkins

Amplified Bible (Zondervan)

Proverbs C12, V11

11) He who tills his land shall be satisfied with bread, but he who follows worthless pursuits is lacking in sense and is without understanding.

Proverbs C13, V15

15) Good understanding wins favor, but the way of the transgressor is hard [like the barren, dry soil or the impassable swamp].

Proverbs: C14, V1 & V6

1) EVERY WISE woman builds her house: but the foolish one tears it down with her own hands.

6) A scoffer seeks Wisdom in vain [for his very attitude blinds and deafens him to it], but knowledge is easy to him who [being teachable] understands.

Common Sense

Mrs. Brown said living righteous brings true correction to one's life. It teaches us how to keep our emotions intact and allows us to stay humbled within our own senses. And be joyful because we have the endurance to be humbled, with true wisdom from the senses of the mind.

Dorothy Mae Pickens Jenkins

Amplified Bible (Zondervan)

Proverbs: C10, V21& V23

21) The lips of the righteous feed many: but fools die for want of wisdom.

23) It is as sport to a fool to do mischief: but a man of understanding hath wisdom.

Job: C28, V28

28) But to man He said, Behold, the reverential and worshipful fear of the Lord-this is Wisdom: and to depart from evil is understanding.

Proverbs: C4, V5

5) Get skillful and godly Wisdom, get understanding (discernment, comprehension, and interpretation), do not forget and do not turn back from the words of my mouth.

Common Sense

Mrs. Blackman had never met anyone that encouraged their own child to leave their spouse and "go" out of the country for a week. And stay with them, knowing just three days earlier the spouse had major surgery. That was the most hurtful and one of the most disappointing things she had ever endured when her husband agreed to go. Now you tell me if we needed anything more than just common "sense" to figure this one out. All that was necessary is common sense and just a little compassion.

Dorothy Mae Pickens Jenkins

Amplified Bible (Zondervan)

Psalm: C77, V9

9) Has God [deliberately] abandoned or forgotten His graciousness? Has He in anger shut up His compassion? Selah [pause, and calmly think of that]!

Psalm: C111, V4

4) He has made His wonderful works to be remembered: the Lord is gracious, merciful, and full of loving commission.

Psalm: C145, V8

8) The Lord is gracious and full of compassion, slow to anger and abounding in mercy and loving-kindness.

Kings: C 10, V7

7) I did not believe it until I came and my eyes had seen Behold, the half was not told to me. You have added wisdom and goodness exceeding the fame I heard.

Common Sense

Mrs. Waters has the quality and behavior of becoming offended and not being offensive when she chooses to at her discretion. These people usually are very sensible people, using a lot of wisdom in their lives. And when they are right in the middle of trouble and trouble-making people. But that's ok because the trouble people need them around to help them keep the peace. The people with discretion are there to help the non- discreet people to uplift their morality and learn some "wisdom". Wisdom is something we have learned to use in today's society for our ethically and "sociable" behavior. Hopefully, we can leave this wisdom behind in our society for our children. And they will feel confident in themselves and become well rounded, excelling human beings.

Dorothy Mae Pickens Jenkins

Amplified Bible (Zandervan)

Job: C12, V13

But only with God are [perfect] wisdom and might; He alone has [true] counsel and understanding.

Job: C121, V16

With Him are might and wisdom; the deceived and the deceiver are His [and in His power].

Job: C12, V3

But I have understanding as well as you, I am not inferior to you. Who does not know such things as these [of God's wisdom and might]?

Job: C12, V1 & V2

THEN JOB answered, No doubt you are the [only wise] people [in the world], and wisdom will die with you!

Common Sense

Mr. C said wisdom is having common sense, good judgement, knowledge, and information based on our good and bad experiences. Having good conduct, with prudent supernatural wise advice, plus proper plans for our lives now and for the future.

Dorothy Mae Pickens Jenkins

Amplified Bible (Zondervan)

Exodus: C31, V3

3) And I have filled him with the spirit of God, in wisdom and ability in understanding and intelligence, and in knowledge and in all kinds of craftsmanship.

Proverbs: C4, V11

11) I taught you in the way of skillful and godly wisdom Which is comprehensive insight into the ways and purposes of God. I have led you in paths uprightness.

Proverbs: C10, V10

10) He who winks with the eye [craftily and with malice] causes sorrow, the foolish of lips will fall headlong but he who boldly reproves makes peace.

Colossians: C2, V3

3) In Him all the treasures of [divine] wisdom (comprehensive insight into the ways and purposes of God) and [all the riches of spiritual] knowledge and enlightenment are stored up and lie hidden.

Common Sense

Troy and Paige are dating at this time in her life and yearn for him, cancel out what she is or anyone else wants for her. She had made the decision to endure whatever it takes because she was only interested in him. And the understanding in him and in his understanding in knowing exactly what he wanted from her. He wasn't mature enough to understand once she made the decision; it didn't make any difference to what his thoughts or fears were because she had digested his life into her physical body. But now, it is a necessity that she kept her mental capability within her. Because she knew there was going to be some unpleasant disappointments, disaffection, and disallowed things going down this road. No matter where it leads them, the way he lived his life was going to become her way of living too. So she must keep her dignity and prerogative in control because there is going to be an enormous amount of conflict. What is amusing is he doesn't have a clue to what degree his life is going to change.

What is amazingly transparent she recognizes there is no her without him. But it's outrageous that he is clueless to the sensibility of the real truth. His fear will not allow him to be conscious of how he feels about her, which was unconditional love; she knew she has enough grace in her heart which gives her confidence to know it is a necessity and reality to stay connected to the relationship. Of course, I'm talking about her, because as subtle as she is, she could not allow him to disconnect from her because the relationship would end. And then it would not matter how much prerogative and dignity she tried to put into it. Common sense will tell her it would have been no use to try to save it. That is why it was a necessity to have a loyal, confident friend in her life, which was very difficult but essential to have. Her friend never knew or experienced such an authentic, credible, ethical woman in this lifetime as her, who was willing to accept all consequences with no regrets. And handle it all with endurance and a lot of frivolous. Within all of this nonesense going on, she manages to keep her focus. Knowing full well his complications will not change, he will not suddenly develop a quiet composure. So they grew into each other and together lived happily with a medium amount of narcissistic behavior.

Dorothy Mae Pickens Jenkins

Amplified Bible (Zondervan)

Colossians: C3, V13)
13) be gentle and forbearing with one another, and if one has a difference (a grievance or complaint) against another, readily pardoning each other: even as the Lord has [freely] forgiven you, so must you also [forgiven].

Proverbs: C4, V7 & V8
The beginning of Wisdom is: get Wisdom (skillful and godly Wisdom)! [For skillful and godly Wisdom is the principal thing] And with all you have gotten, get understanding (discernment, comprehension, and interpretation) [James1:5].

Prize Wisdom highly and exalt her, and she will exalt and promote you: she will bring you to honor when you embrace her.

1 John: C4, V18
18) There is no fear in love [dread does not exist], but full-grown (complete, perfect) love turns fear out of doors and expels every trace of terror! For fear brings with it the thought of punishment, and he

who is afraid has not reached the full maturity of love not yet grown into love's complete perfection].

Common Sense

Mr. Fred said, "We are intelligent human beings We are capable of providing for ourselves and our families We can make good decisions regarding our families, friends, business associates in this society".

Dorothy Mae Pickens Jenkins

Amplified Bible (Zondervan)

Ecclesiastes: C9, V11
11) I returned and saw under the sun that the race is not to the swift nor the battle to the strong, neither is bread to the wise nor riches to men of intelligence and understanding nor favor to men of skill, but time and chance happen to them all [Ps 33:16-19, Rom 9:16].

Luke: C2, V47
47) And all who heard Him were astonished and overwhelmed with bewildered wonder at His intelligence and understanding and His replies.

Revelation: C17, V9
9) This calls for a mind [to consider that is packed] with wisdom and intelligence [it is something for a particular mode of thinking and judging of thoughts, feelings, and purposes]. The seven heads are seven hills upon which the woman is sitting.

1 Corinthians: C5, V18
18) Let no man deceive himself if any man among you seers eth to be

wise in this world, let him become a fool, that he may be wise.

Common Sense

Jarvis said, "We must keep our composure, and we can by using laughter for many things to hide our true feelings and get through embarrassing situations" Sometimes in our hearts, we become angry at ourselves and others because of the embarrassment. And to get ourselves through the embarrassment, we laugh it off. Some people can insult our intelligence so badly, we will laugh or smile to keep from becoming hurt, violent or both. Because there is nothing else we can do or should do other than play it off or make matters worse by acting like them, and that doesn't solve anything. Laughter or a smile is the best medicine for the solution; when we have been versed in your heart, you will be able to handle any situation that comes before you in your life.

Dorothy Mae Pickens Jenkins

Amplified Bible (Zondervan)

Job: C8, V21
21) He will yet fill your mouth with laughter and your lips with joyful shouting.

Proverbs: C14, V13
13) Even in laughter the heart is sorrowful, and the end of mirth is heaviness and grief.

Ecclesiastes: C2 V2
I said of laughter, It is mad and of pleasure What does it accomplish?

Ecclesiastes: C7, V3

Sorrow is better than laughter for the sadness of the countenance the heart is made better and gains gladnessCor7:10].

CHAPTER 6

CONSEQUENCE OF DECEPTIVE BEHAVIOR

Common Sense

We are talking about dignity well (Maggie) has none, she shows the manner of being dignified, but dignity is not in her heart. Dignity is not something to be used for our convenience. When we want to win someone's confidence so we may use them when the opportunity presents itself.

These people become evil because they become dissatisfied with themselves because they don't have no respect for themselves. And that makes them realize they don't have any dignity about themselves at all. Then they start blaming others for treating them a certain way. When they brought it all on themselves on how they treated others. And their interaction with other people in our society left these people with a high opinion of themselves. But do to how they have treated us and others in your presents and in the presents of others whether they were in a professional setting or not. Or one on one, they always wanted to be the center of attention. But when they saw it wasn't getting them what they wanted, then that's when they try and get all dignified. When they already know they don't have not one piece of "dignity" in that whole little raggedy body of theirs. Now they are so angry they start to lash out at everybody. And about that time, even if we are saints, we see that we just can't take this anymore. But there is always one, or two people willing to confront her about her "bad" behavior. And it all goes right back to her not having dignity in herself but expecting others to give her respect, when she doesn't even have any respect for herself. As mama grand would say, you act like a fool, you will be treated like a fool.

Dorothy Mae Pickens Jenkins

Amplified Bible (Zondervan)

Psalm: C75, V5
5) Lift not up your [aggressive] horn on high, speak not with a stiff neck and insolent arrogance.

Proverbs: C8, V35
35) For whoever finds me [Wisdom] finds life and draws forth and obtains favor from the Lord.

Proverbs: C9, V10 & V13
10) The revenant and worshipful fear of the Lord is the beginning (the chief and choice part) of Wisdom, and the knowledge of the Holy One is insight and understanding.

13) The foolish woman is noisy: she is simple and open to all forms of evil, she [willfully and recklessly] knows nothing whatever [of eternal valve].

Common Sense

Nolan is a deceiver, and other men like him have a high opinion of themselves, and they are very particular to whom they date. It's almost always a very attractive woman who has no intention of being honest with them as to how he wants this relationship to go. But in his mind, he wants to be treated with gratitude and respect. And in the meantime, he will keep her on an emotional roller coaster. These people are very careful to choose the individual with a particular, very easy-going personality. They have the wisdom to whom they choose to date or just to sleep with; they are equipped to tell them exactly what they want to hear. These men use all kinds of deceptions to make her feel compassion for him. Such as stories saying my mother locked me in the basement and closet when I was a child. And leaving me in the house by myself, and at the same time, he is consuming her with his affections. And listening to her to see if she has any delusional traits, and if so, what are they? And now he sees her weakness and vulnerabilities. And realizes this is a perfect time to bring on the compassion hard and heavy. Hoping he can bring full satisfaction to her soul, but in the beginning, he was fixated on putting his best foot forward. Treating her excellently on everything, but that's just a ploy working for him that he becomes obsessed with and allows himself to become constantly preoccupied with someone else. And then the table turns to his way of life and the way he lives it. And will not allow her to devote any of her time to anyone but him. And if she did, he would become destructive, unpleasant and violent to her emotional and physical being. Which led to bringing other people into her life and the law enforcement in. And once that happens, she is putting herself at a disadvantage where other people will control her life. Now she starts to think this is the same road I have been down before and starts to blame someone else for her mess. She starts to lie to herself, saying her parents are to blame for her raggedy mess up life. When she knows that is not true, but now she is willing to use her good common sense. And she knows now she has to make a better life for herself and stop allowing herself to be used. Because if she just takes a moment and examines her mind, she will come to a decision to let go and help herself repair her heart. Rightly so, and only then will she set out to live a happy, peaceful, successful life. Let go of that narcissistic thinking and start to think with some wisdom with a plan in mind for herself.

Dorothy Mae Pickens Jenkins

Amplified Bible (Zondervan)

Romans: C3, V13, V14, V17, & V18

Their throat is a yawning grave; they use their tongues to deceive (to mislead and to deal treacherously). The venom is beneath their lips [Ps 529: 140: 31 Their mouth is full of cursing and bitterness [Ps 107].

And they have no experience of the way of peace [they know nothing about peace, for a peaceful way they do not even recognize]. 59:7 8]. There is no [reverential] fear of God before their eyes [Ps 36:1].

Common Sense

Mr. Adam was a very abusive man, there are many different abusive behaviors, and he had them all, bad language, harsh treatment, insulting and serious scolding. He also had such a disapproval attitude of expressing his opinion about something or someone. He became abusive by his mannerism and the way he talked to people. He became abusive of his privileges, which led him to lose an opportunity for education and a better life for himself. And his mannerism tells a lot about his behavior, whether it is disapproval or approval. He didn't want a solution because he wanted to hide his abusive behavior because he was ashamed of it. But his wife knew, and she doesn't have the right to consent to wrongdoing. She thought that he is an abuser; it will ruin his job, good standing in the community and in society.

And she knew there would not be any consequence behind anything he did bad or indifferent. And she can't be a part of that because if so, it would make her as bad as he is; she would become an enabler. Now you see how common sense is very important and how we can be left with a sense of importance and righteousness.

Dorothy Mae Pickens Jenkins

Amplified Bible (Zondervan)

1 Peter: C3, V16 & V17 & V18

[And see to it that] your conscience is entirely clear (unimpaired), so that, when you are falsely accused as evildoers, those who threaten you abusively and revile your right behavior in Christ may come to be ashamed [of slandering your good live].

For [it better to suffer [unjustly] for doing right, if that should be God's will, than to suffer [justly] for doing wrong. For Christ [the Messiah Himself] died for sins once for all, the Righteous for the unrighteous (the Just for the unjust, the Innocent for the guilty), that He might bring us to God. In His human body he was put to death, but He was made alive in the spirit.

Proverbs: C9, V7

7) He who rebukes a scorner heaps upon himself abuse, and he who reproves a wicked man gets for himself bruises.

Common Sense

Coy is already in deep withdrawal in his life, and he is a very troubled young man. The reality is he has suffered from the fact of not having full-time parents in the home, and he has grieved for his father. Most of the time, it affects the man child more than the female child. The man child goes through so many mental states of mind, it brings a lot of anxiety, insecurity, shame, hostility to him. And all of this leads to making bad choices because he feels like his father didn't love him enough to stay around and be in his life. it's as if he wasn't worth loving, and he feels there was no justification for his father leaving him, and there isn't. Any reasonable, fair-minded, common sense person shouldn't have left his son. There is no way that child will escape from some tremendous problems in his life. Growing up into his adult life was very hard for him because he got into trouble with the law and ended up in prison. In his early twenties, this particular young man went to prison for killing a man in the early nineteen hundred`s. This is a young man that is in withdrawal, grieving with no wisdom and grieving from a lack of parenting from his father. A mere child in prison feeling all along and not caring for his emotions which are at the bottom of the barrel. Right now, he is barely capable of sustaining himself despite the fact he is a decent human being in prison. His endurance will call for all the courage that he has stored up in his heart. Now, look at what you have gotten yourself into, a prison. You know your behavior has got to change to be more inline towards the decent human being you were raised to be and who you really are. Now think about what got you into this predicament in the first place. There is nothing more precious than having the satisfaction of having the truth told to yourself. You must admit the influence of your grandparents raising you is still with you. You must rise up to the beliefs of your heart because that's all you have right now. And right now, it is what is essentially important as long as you are in prison. Please do accept it because this is going to be your home for quite some time. This is the perfect time to rely on truth and common sense. There is no time for a half-truth and not accepting reality. There is simply no place for it here; you must be completely honest with yourself and with everyone around you to make it out of here. There is no way that my sanity is not going to be challenged in this place. But what I have working for me is the ability to reach back and rely on my faith. And what mama and grandfather used to say to me the proof is in the putting. And will come out in you, so get your mind out of the gutter and allow yourself to be suitable for these conditions. To whatever they may turn out to be, my suitability will become a life lesson to my stay in this place of imprisonment. And walk out of here with my dignity, a solid mind and full of forgiveness. And caring for others more than I care about myself. In all reality, I must say I'm deeply grateful to my grandparents for teaching me right from wrong and staying committed to the endurance of it all. Within 10 years, he was out of prison.

Dorothy Mae Pickens Jenkins

Amplified Bible (Zondervan)

Genesis: C39, V20 & V21 & V23

And Joseph's master took him and put him in the prison, a place where the state prisoners are confined: so he was there in the prison.

But the Lord was with Joseph, and showed him mercy and loving -kindness and gave him favor in the sight of the warden of the prison.

23) The prison warden paid no attention to anything that was in [Joseph's] charge, for the Lord was with him and made whatever he did to prosper.

James: C1, V3

3) Be assured and understand that the trail and proving of your faith bring out endurance and steadfastness and patience.

Common Sense

Kinsey is a very obnoxious human being and unhappy in her life up to a point. She feels better within herself when she hurts and misuses others. She doesn't think about the consequences because she assumes there will be none for her. Once she sees it, she pretends that it's ok and she doesn't have to do anything about her diminishing acts. As obnoxious as she is, she is very good at deceiving others. She totally insists on others respecting her, but she doesn't believe she has to necessarily give that same respect back. It is as if she thinks other people are not worth respecting. Because it doesn't add any value to her by treating other people with respect. Even though she demands respect from them, which brings conflict to her and everyone around her. Knowing how she treats people, she still wants people to treat her with respect and loyalty. Now, if we allow ourselves to be treated unethically, it will cause confusion throughout families and our society. This may cause destructive and dysfunctional trouble She has no compassion for others misfortunes. If she does decide to throw you a crumb, you'd better be ready to do what she says and when she says. She has to be in control of you; she doesn' have any boundaries, only the ones she sets for you.

Dorothy Mae Pickens Jenkins

Amplified Bible (Zondervan)

Psalm: C71, V6 & V7

Upon You have I learned and relied from birth: You are He Who took me from my mother's womb and You have been my benefactor from that day My praise is continually of You.

I am a wonder and surprise to many, but You are my strong refuge.

Psalm: C109 V3 & V4

They have compassed me about also with words of hatred and have fought against me without a cause.

In return for my love they are my adversaries, but I resort to prayer.

CHAPTER 7

ENVY AND BEING JEALOUS OF ONE ANOTHER

Common Sense

Mrs. Mae Ella said we have to use discerning with people that come into our lives that have this polite apologetic behavior. They want you and others to think things are fine. When they know they are being deceitful, and the truth is they are confused, conceited people. They start to resent others because of the truth about themselves and their life. Then they start to blame others, because the real problem is, they are envious and always have been the envy of your life. They don't realize where and how each other lives. And who we live with and who we are married has nothing to do with our relationship. After some time has passed, some of them do come to a decision of regret (How do I know?) because it's written all over their face every time we see them. We think they just might want to apologize and pick-up our long term relationship that had been so precious to us for years. (But oh no), by this time, they are even more resentful and have lost all of their dignity. Now that's if they ever had any in the first place. what they do now), they become furious, acting out of frustration, in their mind. Still wishing secretly in their heart they would love to be the person you are, but they just can't. They remain opinionated and become an embarrassment to them self and everyone around them, with delusional believes and is still living in denial.

Dorothy Mae Pickens Jenkins

Amplified Bible (Zondervan)

1 Corinthians: C3, V3

3) For you still [unspiritual, having the nature] of the flesh [under the control of ordinary impulses]. For as long as [there are] envying and jealousy and wrangling and factions among you, are you not unspiritual and of the flesh, behaving ourselves after a human standard and like mere unchanged men?

Galatians: C5, V26

26) Let us not become vainglorious and self-conceited, competitive and challenging and provoking and irritating to one other, envying and being jealous of one another.

Proverbs: C3, V31

31) Do not resentfully envy and be jealous of an unscrupulous, grasping man, and choose none of his ways [Ps 37:3; Prov 24:1].

Proverbs: C14, V30

30) A calm and undisturbed mind and heart are the life and health of the body, but envy, jealousy, and wrath are like rottenness of the bones.

Common Sense

Mrs. Katelin met and admired a young lady named Mary who was overwhelmed by how other people around her were doing. Everyone around Mary was doing very well, and she was very happy for them. But she had trouble believing she would ever have that kind of success. Mary is feeling like everyone is doing well except her, and she is feeling a little bit jealous. Which is leaning into temporary darkness, and she doesn't know how to stop these feelings. And she starts to think this is the way her life is going to be forever. And she will never have a life like her closest friend, not realizing she already has that and all the prosperity that goes right along with it. Mary is just soaked up into feeling sorry about her circumstances, and she doesn't see the good in any of the friends that love and care about her. It's hard for her to think of anything and anyone other than herself because she is so self-absorbed. Not knowing she's hurting herself and others by living such a selfish life, not realizing her happiness depends on her own self-worth. Mary felt out of place with everyone, including herself, most of the time, and she knew this wasn't normal behavior. But it seems she just could not pull herself together, but only for a short period of time. So she felt she could not be around any of her friends without becoming envious and jealous of them. She is not wanting to continue to be around them without feeling sorry for herself. Mary thought it would be better for everyone, including herself if she just didn't come around anymore. She allows her insecurities to take her away from her family and friends. With no confidence in herself or anyone else, she just went on with her private matters and her little secrets. Not trusting anyone or herself and having no concern that she can't live like this the rest of her life without making a change. But if Mary doesn't make a change or get help, she will go insane. She had to come to an understanding that she is no longer going to live that way anymore. She is not going to continue to live her life in solitude and miss out on the very best of her life with family, friends and society

Dorothy Mae Pickens Jenkins

Amplified Bible (Zondervan)

Proverbs: C1, V2

2) That people may know skillful and godly Wisdom and instruction, discern and comprehend the words of understanding and insight.

Proverbs: C2, V2

2) Making your ear attentive to skillful and godly Wisdom and inclining and directing your heart and mind to understanding [applying all your powers to the quest for it]:

Psalm:C18, V25

25) With the kind and merciful You will show Yourself kind and merciful, with an upright man You will show Yourself upright:

Proverbs: C3, V27

27) Withhold not good from those to whom it is due [its rightful owners] when it is in the power of your hand to do it[Rom 13:7 Gal 6:10].

Common Sense

Liza is a person who is not reliable to anything that requires stabilization; it's very hard for her to bring stability into her life. She tends to live for the moment by sitting back and waiting on an opportunity to zero in on someone at an approachable time. So she may benefit herself when she is in conversation with other people to obtain information, so she may benefit from it in the meantime. She tends to embellish her lifestyle to how expensive everything is to what she does, where, and the places she has been. Liza is one of the most unreliable people anyone will ever meet, but she continues to try to impress. Because her plan is to impress everyone around her. As one of the most intelligent human beings on earth, she is a very passive-aggressive person. Thinking everybody owes her something and thinks she is a gift to the world. And she must give herself to everyone because she feels nobody can resist her. Liza feels like she must give physical pleasure to others because they would not be able to live without the pleasure of her passion. She simply isn't a good, responsible person because she is so selfish and too busy trying to pleasure herself with everyone that she comes in contact with. And in the end, she becomes an irresponsible human being to others and herself. And from the truth and reality of what a good Godly life is, she tends to lean on other's emotions. And trying to make you feel like you must live her way of life. And let go of your own way of life, which would be disingenuous to yourself.

Dorothy Mae Pickens Jenkins

Amplified Bible (Zondervan)

Isaiah: C44, V25

25)am the Lord] Who frustrates the signs and confounds the omens [upon which the false prophets forecasts of the future are based] of the [boasting] liars and makes fools of diviners, Who turns the wise backward and makes their knowledge foolishness[1 Cort:20].

Romans: C2, V20

20) You are] a corrector of the foolish, a teacher of the foolish, a teacher of the childish, having in the Law the embodiment of knowledge and truth--

Romans: C3, V14 & V16

14) Their mouth is full of cursing and bitterness [Ps 10:7] Destruction [as it dashes them to pieces] and misery mark their way.

CHAPTER 8

JEALOUSY AND ANGER

Common Sense

Roger is a black man who shot his brother at a nightclub because he said his brother should have been at home with his wife. And he had no business being out in a nightclub, when he had such a good wife at home waiting for him to come home. Mrs. Foreman said who he thinks it is ok to take someone's life because he feels like his brother should be at home with her. Mrs.Foreman would think he would make an appointment with his brother and sit down and talk to him. Not come to a club where he is and walk out behind him and say, you need to go home to your wife; she is waiting for you. The brother turns around to face his brother, and he shoots him in his stomach the brother falls to the ground right beside his car. While reaching for his car door to get in his car, his brother killed him. His full blood brother is the same Mother and Father. He spent weeks in the hospital fighting for his life. In the end, he didn't make it, and he died. The brother went to jail for a short while; no, he didn't go to prison; he got out of jail within weeks and continued to live his life. Why was this crime committed? I will tell you why. Out of pure jealousy. But jealous or no jealous, he had no right to take another person's life. He was a human being, someone God created, and he was his brother.But we want Americans to accept us as equal when we don't accept each other as equal to one another. But we want others to do something that we are not doing for ourselves and can't you see, it is not working for us. Yes, America

99

knows we are capable of doing better, and we know it too, but we are just not doing it. Listen, when did we become afraid of hard work? We are asking Americans to have our back when we don't even have each other's back. Where are our common-sense people? I will tell you where it is; you throw it away because you thought you didn't need it because we have a degree. Now didn't Mama Grand tell us to go and get your education, but don't forget your common sense. And to use your common sense right along with your education, but you didn't. That tells me you didn't keep the good common sense you already had; that was a gift. And now you are dumber now than you were before you went out and got an education. You through your common senses away. Why should anyone help us? When we don't have sense enough to keep what was given to us. And why do we keep talking about common senses over and over again? Because we act as if we still don't understand, and I don't want to fail you or myself, we have to stop this narcissistic behavior. It will lead to destruction and death.

Dorothy Mae Pickens Jenkins

Amplified Bible (Zondervan)

Proverbs: C27, V4
Wrath is cruel and anger is an overwhelming flood, but who is able to stand before jealousy?

Deuteronomy: C29, V20
The Lord will not pardon him, but then the anger of the Lord and His jealousy will smoke against that man, and all the curses that are written in this book shall settle on him: the Lord will blot out his very name from under the heavens.

Job: C5, V2

For vexation and rage kill the foolish man: jealousy and indignation slay the simple.

Proverbs C6, V34

For jealousy makes [the wronged] man furious: therefore he will not spare in the day of vengeance [upon the detected one).

Common Sense

This is a little sister's story about a man everyone called him Mr. Eufaula; in fact, he was from a town named Eufaula In his adult life, he moved to the largest city in Oklahoma and became an entrepreneur of a small nightclub. He also worked outside the club on a totally different job, Mr. Eufaula's wife ran the club daily in the daytime hours. And one day Mr. Eufaula walked into his club late evening. And saw another man behind the counter with his arm around his wife's neck. Little sister was sitting there in one of the booth's with her fiance, who was the son of the man that was hugging Mr. Eufaula's wife She heard him say, I told you to stay from behind the counter of the place of business and keep your hands off my wife. The man started laughing very loudly, walking out from behind the counter, walking up to Mr. Eufaula. As Mr. Eufaula turned to walk away, the man kicked him in the buttock Mr. Eufaula turned back to the man and said. I told you to stay away from the counter and my wife.

I'm going to get my gun and come back and kill you. The man simply turns back behind the counter and starts hugging and kissing Mr. Eufaula's wife. The man and Mr. Eufaula's wife, it seems they were enjoying each other. Then the man walked over to the table where his son and his son's fiancee were and said to his son, I want you to watch that door And soon as he comes in that door, you shoot him, cause son he's going to be watching me, so you will have a good shot at him. Here's the gun; put it in your pocket, and when that door comes to open, you be ready. The son said, okay, daddy, I got it, I got it, daddy. The daddy said okay and looked his son in the face, and gave him a couple of slaps on his hands. And said, you got it, the son said yeah!! yeah!! I got it, and his father turned and walked back behind the counter. The son's fiancee stood up abruptly and said to him, let's get out of here, and the son said. I am not going anywhere I got to be here for my daddy, and the fiance said, "well I'm leaving". And the son said, sit your ass down, you not going no damn where and he grabbed her arm and held on to her. Less than five minutes later, the door flew open, the son and fiancee were still standing, the man came out from behind the counter and walked toward the door. It was Mr. Eufaula with a sawed-off shotgun; he shot the son immediately the son tried to shoot him, but the gun fell to the floor. The father fell to the floor at the same time Mr. Eufaula started talking to the son, and "little sister". Brother Pick, who was squatting down behind the cigarette machine with two guns and Mr. Eufaula said, "Little Pick, kick that gun over here," which little Pick did. He then told little Pick to lay his other gun on top of the cigarette machine, then come out and walk out the side door. Mr. Eufaula said I know your daddy, they called him tender foot, and little Pick did exactly what Mr. Eufaula said. And as he was walking out the door, he told his sister to do as he said. Then Mr. Eufaula said to little Pick don't you come back, and little Pick said, oh no, sir, I won't come back. After Mr. Eufaula saw that little Pick was out the door. He started talking to the fiancee, who he called little sister; he said he was down, put your arms around little. Henry the son and took him out the side door I'm not going to hurt you; like I said, I know your daddy or "tender foot". So go on out the side door and take little Henry right along with you. And Mr. Eufaula kept saying, not going to hurt you, and that's all she could hear until she got completely outside and the door slammed shut. She looked down at Henry's leg; it was so shambling it was dragging the ground, blood running from it. Then little sister felt something running down her legs; she looked down on herself and saw she was bleeding too. At the same time, she is still holding on to Henry then she is started to feel weak. About the time she looks up, there is an ambulance, and she doesn't remember anything else until she wakes up in the hospital. Hearing voices saying no, don't move her, take him upstairs, and leave her here, if we move her, she will lose this baby. Leave her here, we have to stop the bleeding, and little sister said, save my baby, please save my baby. The doctor said, we will save you and your baby, and everything will be alright, so rest now. Little sister woke up the next morning; the first thing she did was grab her stomach and said thank you, God She opened her eyes, and there was a doctor standing there saying. I told you everything was going to be okay. You and your baby boy are just fine, and we are going to keep you all for a little while just as a precaution, but baby and mom are just fine Little sister said, thank you, doctor, thank you, thank you for saving my baby, and the doctor said, you are so welcome But don't you mean you and your baby, because there would be no baby without mama. Yes, that's right, what I mean, is thank you doctor, but how are my fiance and his father?

The doctor said, okay, you just rest because you and the baby need all the rest possible, the bleeding has stopped. But you have to lie still for you, and that baby boy needs to rest now, I will be back to check on you. When the doctor came back later, she asked him how is my fiance and his father were doing? The doctor said, they are okay; we need you to concentrate on you and that baby right now. You lost a lot of blood, so let us make sure you and the baby are alright.

Little sister woke up within the next day or two, and she asked how is my baby doing? He is good enough, and we think maybe you can go home within a couple of days. Little sister let out a sigh of relief, smiled, and said thank you doctor. The doctor said, you are certainly welcome. As the doctor walked away, he looked back and said the nurses would bring you some food Little sister said, okay, thank you, but how are my fiance and his father? As I said before, the doctor said they are fine; we are more concerned about you and that baby right now, okay, she said, okay. The next day the doctor let mom and baby go home, providing that her uncle and aunt said they would make sure she stayed on bed rest for at least three more days. So little sister went home with her uncle and aunt, who didn't say anything or talk about her fiance and his father. Once little sister was up and walking around, she asked her uncle and aunt how is her fiancee and his father doing? They said your fiancee is good, and they are going to release him to come home in a day or two. But his daddy is not doing too well, and he is asking to see you but let's not think about that right now. You and that baby are the most important things in our lives right now. Let's concentrate on getting you stronger, and then you can think about if or when you want to see your father in law. And you know, as soon as they let this baby's daddy out, he's going to come right over here. So are you okay with that? She replied, yes, it's okay, alright, I'm okay. But she could still hear that voice in her mind saying, don't you move, lay completely still. Because you still can abort your baby, do you understand? She said, yes, I understand I will not move, just don't let anything happy to my baby. Then she said to herself lay; still, she thought about what her mama grand said to her as she was growing up. When you become a woman, she said you stay out of those bars and nightclubs that are no place for a woman. And her grandmother said to her, I want you to use your common sense no matter how much education you get, never leave your common sense behind Meanwhile, her father in law was still in the hospital, and she knew along with everyone else he might not make it. But he keeps telling his son and everyone else he wanted to see little sister, pleading to them to ask her to come to see him but she had already been there less than two weeks ago. She walked slowly into his hospital room and he immediately said, is that you, little sister? She said nothing, and he said, come closer, come he said, she walked slowly across the room up to his bed. He raised his hand, reaching for her, saying, come let me touch you, give me your hand, and he touched her stomach. He said, my grandson. And then his hand just started to slide off of her stomach, he said something else, and she thinks he said, I'm sorry From the movement of his mouth, she thinks he said sorry, but she never heard the actual words. I' m sorry she could not move for a moment she watched his mouth movements and was trying to read his lips. Unfortunately, he passed away with his hand on his little sister's stomach, saying that my grandson Mr. Eufaula went to prison for two to four years; he committed murder because his heart was hurting and his pride was stripped away from him. And the man that lost his life, he was a womanizer, user, and bully. So you tell me if common sense had been used, this could have turned out totally different Instead, the baby boy's father got shot in the knee, and he had a bad knee for the rest of his life. The mother almost lost her life, and the baby and the grandfather lost his life. And Mr. Eufaula went off to prison, but unfortunately, he only got two to four years for taking a man's life.

Dorothy Mae Pickens Jenkins

Amplified Bible (Zondervan)

Exodus: C20 & V17

You shall not covet your neighbor's house, your wife, or his manservant or his maid servant, or his ox, or his donkey, or anything that is your neighbor's [Luke 12:15, Col 3:5].

Jeremiah: C8 V21

21) For the hurt of the daughter of my people am I [Jeremiah] hurt: I go around morning: dismay has taken hold on me.

Proverbs: C5, V19 & V20

Let her be as the loving hind and pleasant doe [tender, gentle, attractive] let her bosom satisfy you at all times, and always be transported with delight in her love.

Why should you, my son, be infatuated with a loose woman, embrace the bosom of an outsider, and go astray?

Common Sense

Mr. McCoy said, "Feeling grief is losing loved ones by death or accident." By witnessing something atrocious such as people suffering or starving to death, who don't have food to eat or a place to stay. And in today's society, we can't do anything or very little about it. And we bear a real sad feeling because of a physical beating, or we have wronged someone by something we did or didn't do.

Dorothy Mae Pickens Jenkins

Amplified Bible (Zondervan)

II Corinthians: C7, V9

9) Yet l am glad now not because you were paired but because you panned Into repentance [that turned you to God] for you felt a grief such as God meant you to feel so that nothing you might suffer loss through us or harm for What we did.

Romans: C9, V2

2) That I have bitter grief and incessant anguish in my heart.

Proverbs: C14, V13

13) Even in laughter the heart is sorrowful and the end of mirth Is heaviness and grief.

Revelation: C21, V4

4) God will wipe away every tear from their eyes and death shall be no more neither shall there be anguish (sorrow and mourning nor grief nor Pam any more for the old conditions and the former order of things have passed away [Isa 8, 35 10].

Common Sense

Devon was not only a threat to us; he was a threat to himself and society. Grandmother Jessica had fixed a family dinner at her home. Marie, a family member, walked into the room, Devon jumped up quickly from the couch, saying I will kill you for taking my boys away from me. Marie stopped firmly dead in her tracks because Devon had startled her, and she was frightened. But not frightened enough that she ran away because at that moment, she saw another family member turn quickly toward Devon. And at the same time grandmother, Jessica had made it back into the room, and she was saying Devon, what are you doing? That is not who you think it is. That is our family member. Marie, that is not your Aunt Geraldine remember she is dead. Grandmother Jessica and the other young man grabbed Devon, saying to him, calm down don't you do that to Marie; she is our family. She had nothing to do with your boys being taken from you Marie was feeling hurt and confused when grandmother Jessica walked back to her and said, sit down, baby, are you alright? She said that's Devon, and he is not well. Then the young man said, you can't do that, Devon, you frightened her; that's my cousin "Mom," tells him she is our cousin and tell him that is "wrong," tell him. Devon just kept repeating, I'll kill her; she took my boys from me. Grandmother Jessica said Devon, you sit yourself down and calm yourself because you can not act like that. And if you do continue to act out, then I can't come and get you for our family summer dinner visits anymore Devon, do you understand what I am saying? In the meantime, everyone is just sitting and looking at how grandmother Jessica was talking and consulting with Devon Then, grandmother Jessica turned to the young Marie and said, baby, you alright? Marie said, yes, I'm okay; then grandmother Jessica said l will explain everything to you later after I take Devon back to the facility. Marie said okay, and grandmother Jessica said there are many misconceptions about all of this, but one thing is for sure he is a very highly disturbed man. I will tell you the truth about everything that I know and not about what somebody else told me, okay Marie said okay, and grandmother Jessica said the moral of this story is we don't have to be around or associate with this kind of behavior. After that episode grandmother, Jessica said, you will not be exposed to that kind of behavior ever again. As time passed, Marie and grandmother Jessica spent a lot of time together. And in the meantime grandmother, Jessica would explain to Marie how it came to be that Devon became like he is Devon, an alcoholic, was very mean to his wife, and he was taken to an institution, but he only stayed for a little while. He was released and came home for about a year but had to be put back in the institution. Devon lost all control of his life and spent the rest of his life in the institution Grandmother Jessica and Marie became close and loved each other dearly. Marie would spend lots of time with grandmother Jessica, and they got to know each other very well.

And they grew to love and care for each other, and most important of all, they respected and trusted each other.

Dorothy Mae Pickens Jenkins

Amplified Bible (Zondervan)

Deuteronomy: C28 & V28

28) The Lord will smite you with madness and blindness and dismay of [mind and] heart.

Ecclesiastes: C1, V17

17) And I gave my mind to know [practical] wisdom and to discern [the character madness and folly [in which men seem to find satisfaction]: I perceived that this also is a searching after wind and a feeling on it[I Thess 5:21].

Psalm: C103 & V4 & V8

4) Who redeems your life from the pit and corruption Who beautifies, dignifies, and crowns you with loving-kindness and tender mercy.

8) The Lord is merciful and gracious, slow to anger and plenteous in mercy and loving-kindness [James 5:11].

CHAPTER 9

THE STATE OF BEING CONTACTED BY DATING, BLOOD OR MARRIAGE

Common Sense

Mrs. Millsap knew this woman and her husband lived in an apartment together with their three children and they were a very hard working couple. They loved each other very much, but the husband had a problem with being faithful. And he refused to take his wife out with him So one day a family member. Mae asked, why don't you take your wife with you sometime? The husband said I can't do that, so Mae asked him why not? He said because she is a straight-up "bountiful" woman when it comes to her body, she shares it like tomatoes share a vine. And it's embarrassing to me when my wife knows more men than 1 the best way I handle that, is I leave her at home. And anyway I have other people to see, Mae said "what" is wrong with you? That is not right, and why do you cheat? Because 1 want to 1 need this, and 1 need these other people in my life, that's what makes me happy. But that is not fair to "her", your "wife", whose talking about fair life isn't fair. But you don't see me crying about it, so I cheat a little; that's no big deal. Yes, it is said Mae it's a big deal to "her" if it wasn't, she would not go looking for you when you go out and party. I'm afraid she is going to hurt you or someone else real bad one day. She is "dangerous," I said I cheat, 1 didn't say I was going to let her catch me cheating. Let us not talk about it "anymore" I don't want us to ruin our friendship. Okay, I'm afraid for you, one day she is really going to hurt somebody, just let us agree to disagree. The very next weekend she went looking for him, this time she took her gun with her. She found him in the night club with a woman; she pulled out her gun and shot the lady in her head. This happened in the early fifties, and to this day, 2019, as far as anyone knows, the bullet is still in her head Why? Because the doctor said it was too dangerous to remove the bullet, and it's possible she could die. Now you tell "me" this woman had just stopped for "one" minute to think using common sense; this could have turned out amazingly different. His wife turned and said I wasn't trying to kill her; I just wanted to scare her I can't go to our prison, she told her husband. You have to get me out of this. And he did, and she walked away 'Scot free'. What kind of person would go out looking for her cheating "husband" find him with another woman, pull out her gun and point it at another human being, and pull the "trigger". I'll tell you what kind a hurting, angry person that did not value another human being's life "What"? She shot another person in the head because she caught "your husband" cheating on you. And she didn't shoot your husband, but she shot "her". Where is our society now? Is it in the past, or is it still here today in the future.

Dorothy Mae Pickens Jenkins

Amplified Bible (Zondervan)

Psalm: C118, V4
Let those now who reverently and worshipfully fear the Lord say that His mercy and loving-kindness lasts forever.

Proverbs: C6, V 27
Can a man take a tire in his bosom and his clothes not be burned?

112

Proverbs: C2, V14, V15

Who rejoice to do evil and delight in the perverseness of evil.

Who are crooked in their ways, wayward and devious in their paths.

Common Sense

Addie is a young woman that has had her heart broken into many pieces. Meanwhile, she is trying to hold it together and keep it all together for herself and her husband. He doesn't have the maturity to understand that she is holding him. And he doesn't have the sense to recognize it's for him; he doesn't understand that she has his back more than she has her own. Because she knows someone has to be there for him if they are going to get themselves together. They have to be there for each other, and he doesn't get that, which makes it terribly frustrating for her. It's almost as if he's preventing her progress; it's like he's playing around with a barbed wire fence, hoping to get his foot or leg caught in it. So she can come to save him from himself, and at the same time, she's already showing up for him. And he can't see it until his foot or leg is caught in the barbed wire. He needs to take the time and look back and see how many times she has gotten him out of the barbed wire without a scratch on his entire body. It seems men are

not qualified to carry as much baggage as women because we would not be their help, mate, if that was true. If we as women would stop a minute and remember to be reasonable about what we are supposed to do for our spouses or significant others. It will become easier for us by being more compassionate women. But in the meantime, don't allow our personal feelings to become secondary because the intent is for us to treat each other equally. And not allow us to make small talk of each other. It is of the utmost importance to trust each other, and then we will learn to put our trust in each other. We will be able to handle any weakness that comes up on us without allowing it to consume us. Remember, we are human beings, and we have to handle things in a respectable way and not allow our human weakness to get in the way. We must realize in all reality, it's all in our mind, and if we stay in control of our mind, we can control our weakness. As women, we must realize why we were put beside our men, and when they fall short, sometimes, we fall with them. Be then we have failed ourselves and the assignment that was especially given to us. We just can't allow ourselves to do that because the intended purpose is to stay mentally and physically strong for each other. But we know a man will always be physically stronger than a woman. However, he needs us for our mind and perseverance that we can give him. Not just for the physical body we have, to communicate to each other's mind and stop putting so much emphasis on the physical body.

Dorothy Mae Pickens Jenkins

Amplified Bible (Zondervan)

Deuteronomy: C1, V12

12) How can I bear alone the weariness and pressure and burden of you and your strife?

Psalm: C38, V4

4) For my iniquities have gone over my head [like waves of a flood]: as a heavy burden they weigh too much for me.

Psalm: C55, V22 & V23

Cast your burden on the Lord [releasing the weight of and He will sustain you: He will never allow the [consistently] righteous to be moved (made to fall, or fail) Pet 5:71].

114

But, you, O God, will bring down the wicked into the pit of destruction: men of blood and treachery shall not live out half their days. But I will trust in, lean on, and confidently rely on You.

Common Sense

Mrs. Mars said, "Don't be the kind of person that neglects, disregards people, nor lacks caring about ruining someone else's life." If we are only involved in a relationship for what we want or can get for ourselves. And that is to become an approved man or woman for your necessity. And with our fever minded slave master mentality. Because you should know better than to treat someone like that, it's as if you don't have sense enough to come out of the rain. And you know you are standing right there getting soaked. But somehow, your little mind is telling you it's okay, and you end up in worse shape than the person you mistreated Why? Because it should be in our nature to take care of one another, especially husbands, wives, children and parents.

Dorothy Mae Pickens Jenkins

Amplified Bible (Zondervan)

Hebrews: C2, V3

3) How shall we escape {appropriate retribution] if we neglect and refuse to pay attention to such a great salvation [as is now offered to us, letting it drift past us forever]'? For it was declared at first by the Lord [Himself], and it was confirmed to us and proved to be real and genuine by those who personally heard [Him speak].

Deuteronomy: C12, V19

19) Take heed not to forsake or neglect the Levite [God's minister] as long as you live in your land.

115

Matthew: C23, V23

23) Woe to you, scribes and Pharisees, pretenders (hypocrites)! For you give a tenth of your mint and dill and cumin, and have neglected and omitted the weightier (more important) matters of the Law-right and justice and mercy and fidelity. These you ought [particularly] to have done, without neglecting the others.

1 Timothy: C4, V14

14) Do not neglect the gift which is in you [that special inward endowment] which was directly imparted to you [by the Holy Spirit] by prophetic utterance when the elders laid their hands upon you[at your ordination].

Common Sense

Tamra said we can not go after someone that's already in love; if we allow ourselves to do that, we need to question ourselves. The fact is you may be just a mere distraction, and you may not get what we want. And what we are doing is sitting ourselves up for tremendous disappointment. That may ruin our life for a short or long time and bring difficulty to someone else's life also. But at the time, we don't realize it because we are so focused on what we want. And not clearly realizing what is happening or thinking about whether it's the best thing for our lives. Because we have not taken it upon ourselves to make the decision based on just our feelings. And knowing they have not made any kind of commitment to us, and knowing they already have made a commitment to someone else. And we didn't take time and allow ourselves to get to know them, or they get to know us. Naive thinking has no room in making a decision that could change our lives forever. But in our minds, we are saying we will do whatever it takes to win them over when someone else already has their heart. And they don't have to lift a finger to do anything as Mama-Grand would say it's a done deal. And if we had given ourselves more time to get to know them, we would have realized we were out of our league anyway. And when we say you could have been out of your league, not to say they are bad people. It just means we weren't the one for them. We usually know when we are out of our league, but sometimes we are too stubborn or ignorant to understand and accept it. That's why we should have a clear understanding of what we have involved ourselves in. Whether we were right, wrong, or in the difference, it's simply all on us. It doesn't matter how deductive we are or have been it will not last. As Mama-Grand would say, we didn't give ourselves time to know each other

Dorothy Mae Pickens Jenkins

Amplified Bible (Zondervan)

1 John: C2, V16 & V26

16) For all that is in the world-the lust of the flesh [craving for sensual gratification] and the lust of the eyes [greedy longings of the mind] and the pride of life [assurance in one's own resources or in the stability of earthly things]-these do not come from the Father but are from the world [itself].

26) I write this to you with reference to those who would deceive you [seduce and lead you astray].

Ephesians: C4, V18

18) Their moral understanding is darkened and their resigning is beclouded. [They are] alienated (estranged, self-banished) from the

life of God [with no share in it: this because of the ignorance (the want of knowledge and perception, the willful blindness) that is "deepseated in them, due to their hardness of heart [to the insensitiveness of their moral nature].

Job: C24, V15

15) The eye of the adulterer waits for the twilight, saying No eye shall see me, and he puts a disguise upon his face.

Common Sense

Mrs. Miles feels Sherlin is one of the most amazing people she has ever met in her life. The thing about this person though is she has problems with being committed to one man. She has said she is only in love with one of them but still does not fully commit to him. My goodness yes, this woman is so confused. She has no intolerability or discipline to be inactive with men. Her extreme mannerism lets anyone know she thinks her body cavity is exceptional. She uses it as if it was an appetizer for an exclusively five-star restaurant. Not only is she ignorant, she likes self-confidence and stupid enough to believe she has no choices over her own body. I would think by her behavior she has no brain or she has caught a horrible infectious disease. And has ruined her brain, so it has left her with nothing to think with. This lady can't sit down to dinner and have a normal conversation without talking about her vagina. She also loves to discuss how her body can make a blind man see, a paralyzed man walk, and a poor man become rich all at the same time. And we know there is no one on earth that can do that. So you see, she gave men total access to enter her womanly private place and let them think they are privileged to enter. And all at the same time, she is relentless in allowing herself to be abused and didn't have sense enough to know it. And is still not accepting and acknowledging what has and is happening to her life. Why? Did this happen to her because she didn't take responsibility for her life and relationships? So you see what can happen to you when you don't think for yourself. Now you are lying here with all of this yellowish-green stuff running out of your body. Something you could have prevented if you just had stopped for a minute, a mere minute. Just a little quality time, but instead, you act as if you had no intellect at all. And now you lay here with your inflamed mind thinking to yourself that you just weren't thinking. You destroyed your own life because you choose not to take responsibility for ruining your life. But you are still being blessed because someone is willing to help you, and all you need to do is listen to them. "Oh", you did listen, but you just didn't hear them? "Oh", I see you didn't have "time" to listen. Sherlin said I was too busy trying to get my college degrees. And one of the most disrespectful things you did is how you mistreated people in a patronizing way, insulting their intelligence.

Dorothy Mae Pickens Jenkins

Amplified Bible (Zondervan)

Romans: C7, V8, V11, V15, & V17

8) But sin, finding opportunity in the commandment [to express itself], got a hold on me and aroused and stimulated all kinds of forbidden desires (lust covetousness). For without the Law sin is dead [the sense of it is inactive and a lifeless thing].

11) For sin, seizing the opportunity and getting a hold on me [by taking its incentive] from the commandment, beguiled and entrapped and cheated me, and using it [as a weapon], killed me.

15) For I do not understand my own actions [I am baffled, bewildered].I do not practice or accomplish what I wish, but I do the very thing that I loathe [which my moral instinct condemned.

17) However, it is no longer I do the deed, but the sin [principle] which is at home in me and has possession of me.

Common Sense

Lilia had to find a man that fit her so she could revive herself. So she may have someone, so she could feel like she could love again. Without hate, if he fit, she thought that was love, but he did fit; he just wasn't ready to love her. He didn't even like that he fit, but only because that gave him leverage to influence her mind in a way, he wanted her to feel and think about him. She didn't understand, but she wasn't in the right frame of mind to even be in a relationship.

Especially when he wanted to be looked at by someone else, and he was very materialist and controlling. It was essential to him that he keep her frustrated so she will not be in charge of her faculties. And that gave him more ability to control her because of what he lacked in himself.

Makes him feel like he must have her under his total control; if he is not in control of her, then that makes him vulnerable to her. He will do anything necessary not to feel vulnerable towards her. So, therefore, he has to know who she talked to and any relationship she has or had with other people, man, woman, professional or personal, whether it was family or none family. And by all means, he must be in charge of all financial accounts It was essential for her to be able to stand a lot of mental pain, but he would use physical pain only if he thought it was absolutely necessary. He tried to stay away from getting physical with

120

her, but the use of physical abuse would subside, but it was always there. In his conceited mind, he only wanted her to excel if he had a life with her. He said she will always land on her feet, with the upper hand in the driver seat calling the shots, stronger than before. She will always bounce back from an abusive relationship whether they were a boyfriend or spouse. We think, why didn't he go to counseling with her as she had asked? He asked why would he go to counseling for something he had planned to do to her in the first place. And it was totally her fault that the relationship turned out the way it did because she made him feel beneath her.

Dorothy Mae Pickens Jenkins

Amplified Bible (Zondervan)

Psalm: C71, V1

1) IN YOU, O Lord, do I put my trust and confidently take refuge: let me never be put to shame or confusion!

Proverbs: C9, V13

13) The foolish woman is noisy she Is simple and open to all forms of evil; she [willfully and recklessly] knows nothing whatever [of eternal value].

Proverbs: C10, V12 & V13

121 Hatred stirs up contentions but love co hers all transgressions

13) On the of him who has discernment skillful and godly Wisdom is found, but discipline and the rod is for the back of him who is without sense and understanding.

Common Sense

Asia, this young woman needed to stop being so naive and stop allowing yourself to become counter productive to yourself. And learn how to become exceptional in how to differentiate the truth from an lie. A percentage of us tend to be too naive for our own good; this woman was just that and tend to believe most of anything she was told. Then one day she met a man she was very attracted to. And her naiveness allowed her to become ignorant in some of her decisions that she made for herself. One year into her dating him, she fell in love with this man and had no control over her feelings for him. Not knowing he had an ex-wife that he was still in love with and didn't tell her he was still in love with her. He stayed in denial and didn't tell his present girlfriend. In his mind, he just couldn't determine if it was wrong, right, in-different, or maybe he just wanted to be selfish for his own pleasures. But the truth is there was personal denial on her part, and she just refused to deal with any of it. She was so in love with him that she thought she would give him some time he would come to love her. As much as he once loved his ex-wife, she was wrong because she could see he was becoming less attentive to her. And more attentive to his fast lifestyle and other women. Which was his way of getting on with his life and getting over his ex-wife. The present girl friend clearly could see that it was tearing him apart. The friend had to stop being so naive and living in self-denial. And accept the fact that the man who had become her fiancé 6 months into their dating was still in love with his ex-wife. It became unacceptable to her, so there she was sitting, waiting on a marriage proposal because none of this was acceptable to her anymore. All of his physical, mental, and energy abilities went to his fast lifestyle and other women. He did propose that they get married, but he did have many affairs before they got married. And the affairs kept going now 2 years into the marriage. It was essential for the second wife to make up her mind to leave or stay and put her desire for him aside because she is not going to put up with this any longer. Oh my God!!, she loved him, so very much only a few people knew how much she really loved him. And only a couple of people that she trusted knew that the break up really messed her up, but she made it through. A lot of obstacles got in the way, but she kicked them out of the way, ran over the ones she couldn't kick out of the way and kept on going. At the time, she felt like her husband was like an octopus with many arms but nothing inside. But he was just like her, only he was in love with his ex-wife. So the reality of it all is there were two people in love but not with each other. One of them was in love with someone else. Now, if you think about it, how could you blame him for being in love and she is feeling the same for him. Now, if you want to blame someone, blame both people for not being brave enough to go their separate ways. He was hurting, trying to get over his first lost love. But she had to start to try and get over him; you know, she thinks he never got over losing his ex-wife to this day. Just as she never completely got over him, and she was waiting on him to love her when he was already in love. So you see, we have to look after our own heart and stop being so naive and ignorant. And living in denial takes hold of your own life, and be responsible for it. And she did come out of her fantasy world and did just fine. Of course, she will never ever love like that again. How is he? And where is he? He is doing well; he is just where he allows himself to go, surrounded by professional people who will take care of him. Because he has taken care of so many people in the past, and now his people will take care of him in the future. How does the second wife feel about him now?

She loves him, just not in love with him; she has her own life now. And she is sending up prayers for him; may he be blessed. Stop let me take you back a bit when she first met him he just wasn't in love with her. He never denied not being in love with his ex-wife; he just refused to tell the present wife. But the disconnect with her, family, friends and associates was very painful. Some thought she had the best of both worlds and in love, but everything was superficial. They pretended to be happy for her, but the truth is they were really jealous of her. And what was so amazing about it she didn't know it at that time. She had very few families and friends who supported her at this time in her life. She was and still is a very plain soft-spoken person, more like her biological mother, the Evangelist. She was so deeply in love with her husband, she had no choice but to leave the marriage.

There were no other quality choices; she just could not give him what he needed to survive. And who in their right mind would remain in a marriage just existing? Neither person wanted to live like that. So she let go and put it in God's hands. That was one of the most difficult things she had to do in her life. She can only describe the way she felt at that time, like a headache, stomach ache, and having a heart attack at the same time. Now you tell me could you stay in pain, of course not and neither could she. His pain was almost as much as hers because he was still in love with his ex-wife. Common sense will tell you this is no way for either of them to live, with the so-called thing we call love. Because love will kill you if you allow it too. She ran out of time to stay and keep loving him when it is so very obvious, he is still yearning for his ex-wife. But he still has a non-physical invitation to her heart.

124

Dorothy Mae Pickens Jenkins

Amplified Bible (Zondervan)

Psalm: C118, V8

8) It is better to trust and take refuge in the Lord than to put confidence in man.

Proverbs: C14, V13

13) Even in laughter the heart is sorrowful, and the end of mirth is heaviness and grief.

Proverbs: C8, V20

20) l [Wisdom] walk in the way of righteousness (moral and spiritual rectitude in every area and relation), in the midst of the paths of justice.

Proverbs: C2, V7

7) He hides away sound and godly Wisdom and stores it for the righteous (those who are upright and in right standing with Him): He is a shield to those who walk upright and in integrity.

Common Sense

Allison, she ran away; this young woman was clueless, inherently sensitive; she was exploited by an older man consistently worming his way into her life; that was his intent from the beginning. He decides he wanted her for his wife and wanted her to have lots of babies for him. And solely learn to trust him and take his advice to heart and do exactly as he says without question. In his mind, he wanted complete control of her mind and emotions. He wanted her to believe in him as an asset to her life, and he didn't see how arrogant he was inside. He wanted her to totally depend on him for everything, and at the same time, he is deceiving her. He knew she wasn't capable of comprehending any of it, and his most important task was to keep her ignorant. Not letting her know he was very malicious, but he wanted her to believe he was the best thing that ever happened to her. Which would keep her very willing and confused. He wanted her to love him and care for him, and trust him no matter how things seem to her. She still could depend on him for anything and everything she needed or wanted. She also wanted to have children with him, and she had two babies within two years. And that's when the missed treatment started, he would scream at her, but he called it talking. Then he started hitting her; she did not panic but kept it inside; she knew she had to start planning to leave him. She knew it was going to take some very careful planning, and it would take some time to get out of there alive. She did survive, but it took her four years to leave. She was left with a mental mine of uncertainties.

Dorothy Mae Pickens Jenkins

Amplified Bible (Zondervan)

Psalm: C56, V3-V4

What time I am afraid I will have confidence in and put trust and reliance in You.

By [the help of God I will praise His word: on God I lean, rely, and confidently put my trust, I will not fear What can man, who is flesh, do to me?

Common Sense

Mrs. Carissa, back in her day she had the encounter of watching timid young women grow And become smitten by the opposite sex; they are traumatized and inclined to be favorable to listen to others by following their given direction and lifestyle. There are men that fall under that same category, but in Carissa's experience, she has met more women who were vulnerable. These women were smitten to the life style of his choosing, and most often, they were attractive or very pretty young women. But one would think it's always the low self-esteem person is the only one who falls into that category which is the so-called norm of it. But there are some women who have the same problems and are very educated. And they have had a very difficult time in this part of their life too. You see, it is not always uneducated that has these undesirable problems that will harm their social life, physical body, and mind. As 'Mama Grand" would say, that's why it's very important we use our common sense when making any decisions. We "must" it's vital that we use our common sense along with our education and always keep our respect and values. In our lives, we learn to respect ourselves and make others do the same. And if you value yourself, you will never let someone else lead you down the wrong road. And most often, these women have not had anyone in their lives that has said I love you or show them what real love is. So they are not so weakminded; they only just look for what they think everyone else has, and that is love but know that is not true for them. And they really don't know what love looks like. So, therefore, once someone says l love you to them, they tend to believe it. And it's not always necessarily true, but they are in denial, so they would rather live in denial and not feel the truth. Because it's too hard for them to accept it at the time, and that's why they sometimes stay in denial. Because it's easier to cope with. Oh yes, I know some would say she is so weak-minded and stupid; no, they are not. They are looking for something that many of us have experienced in our lives, and that's "love". We must hear it, see it, and feel it before we leave this world. The human side of us will not deny ourselves the feeling of those experiences of being loved and being in love. Sometimes they forget about their lives and start giving their all to their person or persons. And in for getting themselves, they tend to forget the children and start to insert her person or persons typical ways or interest into her children. Now don't forget she's already pursuing his life dreams, so now she is delusional, living a false sense of responsibility. It's as if she has a mental disorder, but it's simply because she didn't put any emphasis on anything they said or did unless she had his approval. But she has the potential to overcome this if she "now" can use her common sense. And let her intellect help her accomplish anything and everything that's good for her. These women are decent "people" it's just taken them a little while to find a decent man that will love them like they should be loved. Just remember you have to be able to discern love. Just remember you have to be able to discern love.

Dorothy Mae Pickens Jenkins

Amplified Bible (Zondervan)

I Thessalonians: C4, V4, & V5

That each one of you should know how to possess (control, manage) his own body in consecration (purity, separated from things profane) and honor.

Not [to be used] in the passion of lust like the heathen, who are ignorant

128

of the true God and have no knowledge of His will.

Proverbs; C17, V22

22) A happy heart is good medicine and a cheerful mind works healing, but a broken spirit dries up the bones [Prov12;25: 15:13, 151

Micah: C6, V8

8) He has shown you, O man, what is good And what does the Lord require of you but to do justly, and to love kindness and mercy, and to humble yourself and walk humbly with your God? [Deut 10: 12,13].

Common Sense

This is an Izzy story; she lived on a farm with her grandparents and aunt; it was a very large farm. There was a water well on the land, ponds, creeks, and fruit trees, small and large hills, valleys and rocky roads. This farm sits far, far, out into the woods; our neighbors were at least two to three miles from Izzy and in any different directions. The farm was so spread out at least fifteen to twenty acres. Her aunt would take her on walks with her throughout the woods, but most of the time, it would be where the fruit trees were. There were peach, apple, grape, and persimmon trees and vines. Izzy thought her aunt was the most beautiful woman she had ever seen. She had very fair skin, very pretty long off black hair, and her hair came down to the middle of her back. Izzy had other aunts and uncles, but they didn't stay there; they were in and out. But she remembers one other aunt that was married and lived far away; she would maybe see her once in a year or two. Izzy's daddy would come to see her and her brother once a month, sometimes every two to three weeks, she adored her daddy. When her daddy would come, her face would light up like a

Christmas tree, everyone would say. When he would come to see them, he would take Izzy and her brother into town with him. And he would always go to this one particular cousin's house; he always had a lady friend with him. We were always treated with kindness, and they welcomed us into their home; the cousin was married with children, the children were very nice to us. Izzy would look forward to coming there, she enjoyed being around them, and they enjoyed being around us. Izzy never remembers her aunt coming to the cousin's house with them; sometimes, she would see one of the uncle's there. But the uncle never came with Izzy and her family of four; it was always Izzy and her brother, the lady friend and her daddy. While Izzy and her family were there at the cousin's house, it was always a happy time for their family. Dad, the lady friend, and cousins would play music, dance, eat and have drinks. And there was so much laughter in that's all you could see enjoyment and happiness. That meant a lot to Izzy because she was living without her mother and father in the home. So when her daddy came to see them and take them with him, that meant the world to her. But Izzy didn't see her mother but four or five times in the entire time she was growing up. Their mother was not allowed to see them very often only when daddy said. And he did not say so only about every two to three times a year, but sometimes when we were at our cousin's house he would take Izzy to see her mother. And sometimes, he would leave her there for two to three hours, but the brother never stayed with Izzy. And once the visit was over, he would pick Izzy up and return them back to the farm, then he and his lady friend would drive back to Oklahoma City, where they lived. His lady friend was a pretty lady and always so very nice and kind to us. There were other ladies in his life, but he never brought them around us, only this one lady that was fair skin and taller than him. It "saddened"

Izzy, when her daddy and his lady friend would leave, but she would go to her favorite pound and sit along for a little while. And then she remembered where her aunt was, and suddenly she would feel better racing through the farm looking for her aunt. In less than half an hour, she would always find her, and a big smile would come up on her and her aunt's face. They would walk off together, and they would be in each other's company for thirty minutes to an hour sometime. But soon after, her aunt and the adult man would come, and they would always end up in the fruit garden together. And sometimes that would be the first place Izzy would look, but if they were not there. Izzy would go back to the big peach tree on the side of the house and sit there with her cat, raggedy ann doll, and french bulldog. And the aunt would find her and say, what are you doing, Izzy? Izzy said, playing with my doll; the cat and dog were always with her. Aunt would say, come on, do you want to walk with me? Izzy said yes, mama. Where are we going, aunt? Just come on, I will show you and most often it was going to the fruit garden. And sometimes, it would be a dark brown skin adult man sitting on a log with his guitar. I learned later that his name was Johnnie Harrison Taylor (the singer). Izzy's aunt would have many walks to the fruit garden with her. Izzy could not remember exactly how long her aunt met with Mr. Taylor in the fruit garden, but she felt like it was at least one year. He was always so very nice to Izzy and would bring aunt flowers that maybe he picked them along the way. Izzy remembers he also brought a pretty paper bag with something in it, but her aunt never shared what was in it. Izzy was very young at the time, but imagine in her mind, maybe there was some beautiful lingerie in that bag sometimes. Once Mr. Taylor would arrive at the fruit garden, they would hold hands and kiss each other softly on the lips. But then he would kiss her on her forehead, nose, both cheeks, her eyes, and as he let go of her chin, he would tap her chin and say, I love you. In all of this time, they interact with each other they have this big smile on their face, and Izzy also had a big smile on her face Then Izzy would walk away with the family pit bulldog and play with the butterflies, birds, rabbits, and squirrels. But Slick is the bulldog name and was very protective of our family, but no one ever got hurt, and Slick, the bulldog, never attacked anyone the entire time she was growing up. But Izzy was never out of her aunt's sight, and once the (rendezvous) was over, Izzy and her aunt would return to the house And Mr. Taylor would walk to the trail of woods back to the main road, and sometimes, Izzy and her aunt would walk him to the main road. And then they proceed to turn back, waking through the fruit garden, having some fruit on the way back home. Then one day, Izzy overheard her grandmother say, you will not see this foolish guitar playing 'fool' anymore; men like that are no good; we want you to marry a good man. You are going to start seeing Rev. Goodwater's son; like we told you in the first place, he's a good man. His daddy is a preacher, and that's that no more of this foolishness. As Izzy remember, aunt saw Mr. Taylor about two or three times after that. And aunt never saw Mr. Taylor again, and Izzy loved her aunt very much. But Izzy could see that she was very sad; aunt didn't walk through the fruit garden much anymore. She and Izzy would go to other places in the woods, so now this other man started to come to see her aunt. But no one walked with him in the fruit garden; this man came to the house and sat under the big tree with her aunt. The tree that set out in front of the house, sometimes the entire time he was there. Can't remember if they dated or not; it seems, they just got married right away. And suddenly aunt wasn't there with her anymore, oh my goodness, Izzy was so sad. Now Izzy is feeling so hurt and alone, but after a long while, an aunt came back to the country. She was married to the other gentleman, who used to sit under the tree with her Izzy was so happy to see her aunt again, and her aunt was happy to see her. They gave each other a big hug, and a big kiss on the cheek. She never talked about Mr. Taylor again, until Izzy was all grown Izzy still loved and missed her aunt to this day, may you rest in peace, aunt.

Dorothy Mae Pickens Jenkins

Amplified Bible (Zondervan)

1 Timothy: C3, V4
4) He must rule his own household well, keeping his children under control, with true dignity, commanding their respect in every way and keeping them respectful.

Ephesians: C3, V17
May Christ through your faith [actually] dwell (settle down, abide, make His permanent home) in your hearts! May you be rooted deep in love and founded securely on love.

1 Corinthians: C13, V13
13) And so faith, hope, love abide [faith-conviction and belief respecting man's relation to God and divine things: hope-joyful and confident expectation of eternal salvation: love true affection for God and man, growing out of God's love for and in us] these three: but the greatest of these is love.

Genesis: C29, V20
20) And Jacob served seven years for Rachel: and they seemed to him but a few days because of the love he had for her.

Common Sense

This is Sage's courageous inspiriting couple of the seventies. Sage remembers monogamists "dating" back in the seventies; it seems most women and men were in monogamous relationships whether they were dating or married. Then "Sanford" met "Gwen", and when "Sanford" and "Gwen" started dating, there was nothing and nobody that could keep them apart; they were a monogamous couple. Their generation in the seventies understanding "was" when they were involved in dating or married; the relationship was always monogamist. The generation of women had no desire to date any other way than monogamist. And "Gwen" was precisely one of these women and believed in each other to that fact. But these precious brothers to her and they looked after her because her big brother Alvin P. the second was in prison. At that time, Alvin J. lived about three to four blocks from her, and she saw him two or three times on weekdays and weekends. But Sanford lived across town; she would see him at the very least once or twice every two weeks. And because Sanford and her cousin Alvin J. looked out for Sage. They would occasionally take her out and about with them. At this time, they were just dating; women would swarm around them like bees swarming honey because they were very handsome, decent, and particular men. And when "Sage" was out and about with one of them, the women would become very disturbed and had the audacity to act foolish with Sage. But Sage never would respond to them; she just looked at them with her little quiet, conservative discreet smile. And Sanford would say that's my cousin, and they would say, "yeah "right", then he would repeat himself. And say, "like I said, "this is my cousin Sage, and Sage didn't have anything to say throughout that day or evening to them. But Sage would say under her breath, he didn't want you all for keeps no way. And she would be so glad when he met someone of substance, that he wanted to make a life with and it surely wants to be none of you'll. When Sanford met Gwen. He introduced her to Sage, and he said she is the "one"; she is my lady. Sanford never talked to Sage about a lady like that before, and she knew if he wanted her to meet her, he must be already in love with Gwen or falling in love with her. So later that day, Sanford took Sage to meet Gwen, and she liked her right away, not that it made any difference. Because Sage and everyone else found out she was and is her own person. She is not the one to care about what someone else thinks; the first thing Sanford noticed was how every attractive Gwen was and "still is". From that day, they started to build a relationship with each other with real valves. After meeting Gwen, Sanford's life started to change; he was blown away by her. But it was all for his good and hers; these two people were in love and still are very good for each other. They were generous to each other and still are to this day. This couple is still together, living in a beautiful home they own together, and have had a beautiful happy 40 years of marriage together. Both people have retired, "oh" you thought that was the end well, it's not; I have a few more suitor details to tell. Like Sage said back in the seventies, there were monogamist women who were very popular among those decent, handsome men who wanted a good life. And wanted someone to build and focus on good qualities, which Gwen and Sanford both have. They both were and still are very attractive and consistent compassionate people. The one thing that sage will never "forget" about this couple is the generosity they had for each other and others. And there were many women that came after Sanford, but they couldn't come between him & Gwen. And the same for Gwen, men would try to pursue her to be with them, but she turned them away. There is a lot more I could say about this couple or as an individual, but I will just allow you to take a little peek inside of these two extraordinary people's lives. Allow me to tell you what they taught me; they taught Sage to know she could be successful even if her life was turned upside down at that time. And Sage went on with her life and remarried, and she is very happy, safe and successful Sage wants to tell you all something funny about Sanford. He lived in town, and Sage lived in the country; while growing up, keep in mind he knew nothing about the country. His parents would allow him and his brother to come to stay with Sage in the country for one or two weeks. One morning after we finished breakfast Sanford said, what do we do now, Sage? And she said we go to the field and chop cotton. So all of us and her grandparents went to the fields to chop cotton, and that is just what Sanford did. He chopped down all the cotton and left the weeds, almost a whole row of cotton. My grandparents would have been so angry at any other time, but it was so funny nobody could stop laughing "Oh", you didn't think that was funny? Yes, it's innocently funny "Get it" may God bless and keep both of you. I love you both.

Dorothy Mae Pickens Jenkins

Amplified Bible (Zondervan)

Proverbs: C8, V12, & V21

12) I, Wisdom [from God], prudence my dwelling, and I find out knowledge and discretion [James 1:5].

21) That I may cause those who love me to inherit [true] riches and that I may fill their treasuries.

Joshua: C1, V8 & V9

8) This Book of the Law shall not depart out of your mouth, but you shall meditate on it day and night, that you may observe and do according to all that is written in it. For then you shall make your way prosperous, and then you shall deal wisely and have good success.

9) Haven't I commanded you? Be strong, vigorous, and very courageous But not afraid, neither be dismayed, for the Lord your God is with you wherever you go.

Mrs. Lee Anna said, "Love is strong feelings, with instant pleasure in seeing your face and knowing certain affection is returned to each other" Or just have the pleasures of loving each other and knowing they are loving us the same way with parenting love Parents, love your children, and children, love your parents. As grandparents, it's just in our hearts to love our grandchildren because we have had the experience of loving our own children. When we have that kind of love for our families, it automatically allows us to give love to all generations of our children, with endurance and patients.

Dorothy Mae Pickens Jenkins

Amplified Bible (Zondervan)

Hebrews: C6, V10

For God is not up righteous to forget or overlook your labor and the love which you have shown for his name's sake in ministering to the needs of the saints (His own consecrated people), as you still do.

Philippians: C1, V9

9) And this I pray that your love may abound yet more and more in knowledge and in all judgement.

137

Deuteronomy: C7, V9

9) Know, recognize, and understand therefore that the Lord your God He is God the faithful God. Who keeps covenant and steadfast love and mercy with those who love Him and keep His commandments, to a thousand generations.

Psalm: C5, V7

7) But as for me, I will enter Your house through the abundance of Your steadfast love and mercy. I will worship toward and at Your holy temple in reverent fear and awe of You.

Common Sense

Mr Diesel, this man relic on his total anatomy and his superficial morals to how he lived his life. And choosing how supportive he is going to be to anyone, especially if it's going to benefit him. If you keep this kind of man in your life, you have to recognize who he is very early in the "relationship" if you don't he will lead you straight to the "morgue." But looking at him, he's tall, dark, and handsome, which will put you at a disadvantage. Because you can't see the rotten "evil" person that he is inside. He has so much evil inside of him, but no one could not stand not to look at him. We can't ever get to know these kinds of people in a short period of time. We have to carefully hang on to their every word "and their mannerism" to get to know them well. And in the meantime, they potentially think they are smarter than we are. Only showing themselves how moral they can be. Men like him keep themselves as a fugitive from the moral, righteous people as a society; deep down in their soul, they are afraid of the morally righteous person.

Dorothy Mae Pickens Jenkins

Amplified Bible (Zondervan)

Titus C1, V10,V11 & V12

For there are many disorderly and unruly men who are idle (vain, empty) and misleading talkers and self deceivers and deceivers of others [This is true] especially of those of the circumcision party [who have come over from Judaism].

Their mouths must be stopped, for they are mentally distressing and subverting whole families by teaching what they ought not to teach, for the purpose of getting base advantage and disreputable gain.

One of their [very] number, a prophet of their own, said, Cretans are always lairs, hurtful beasts, idle and lazy gluttons.

Proverbs C26, V11

11) As a dog returns to his vomit, so a fool returns to his folly.

CHAPTER 10

UNDERSTANDING DIFFERENT TYPES OF RELATIONSHIPS

Common Sense

Gina said, "Let us not be overly proud, self-complacent, and not recognize that it is essential to respect the people in our lives and show them appreciation." Whether they show importance to us or not, the point is we don't know how long these people will be in our lives. So treat them in a way that they know we want them to treat us because there is not enough appreciation shown in our relationships with one another. We are blessed human beings but not always the most upright humans; however, we can try to be more caring instead of just rushing through life and not being attentive to our friends and neighbors. Knowing that we are responsible for each other in this world in which we live, There is nothing like spending time with a friend we love, even though that friend isn't who you thought they were. We can't put our standards on someone else because by doing so, we just could lose their friendship forever or have nothing left worth saving. We must start to put more emphasis on our friends and relationships. That's if we want to have loving, lasting relationships with one another. Put more importance into the person and less into yourself, and stop making yourself a little bit more important to yourself than need be. If we don't stop all of this nonsense, we will grow into a narcissistic human being that can not possibly get along with anybody. Instead, we will get stuck out there with all the other narcissistic people who can not possibly get along with anybody, And I assure you that you don't want to live like that. Imagine being out there with everyone just like you with all of these narcissistic behaviors. That's enough to run the devil himself crazy, and he's already extremely evil. Put the devil together with a narcissistic person, and you have got hell on earth, and we already have enough hell on this beautiful earth. Let us strive for love and peace to be extended from one to another like it was intended to be. So our children can grow up more compassionate, understanding, and be a better asset to their families and society.

Dorothy Mae Pickens Jenkins

Amplified Bible (Zondervan)

Romans: C11, V20
20) That is true But they were broken (pruned) off because of their unbelief (their lack of real faith), and you are established through faith [because you do believe]. So do not because proud and conceited, but rather stand in awe and be reverently afraid.

Romans: C12, V13, V14, & V16
Contribute to the needs of God's people [sharing in the necessities of the saints: pursue the practice of hospitality. Bless those who persecute you [who are cruel in their attitude toward you]: bless and do not curse them.

16) Live in harmony with one another; do not be haughty (snobbish, high-minded, exclusive), but readily adjust yourself to [people, things] and give yourself to humble tasks. Never overestimate yourself or be wise in your own conceits. [Prov. 3:7].

Common Sense

Mae lived next door to Mr. & Mrs. Brown; they would tell her it is essential to have an honest, faithful personal relationship with our self living a peaceful life and surrounding ourselves with love, staying away from trouble and troublesome people. As much as possible, keep your eyes on the positive ethical things of life. Be gracious and able enough to deal with any type of person or thing. We have eyes use them to communicate with people, most often, these people are transparent, and we can see right through them. As to what they are thinking, and at the same time, we can be mindful of what they say or do to us. God has put all that is necessary into our minds for us to be able to live happy, successful lives with our family, husband, wife and society with loving relationships. And being the ethical, courageous, loyal, gracious people, we are with eternal optimism. Don't allow other people and their circumstance to bring confused insensate behaviors into our life. We should be discreet and cautious and not allow ourselves to be deceived by people. We all know what appreciation means, so if we carry ourselves in an appreciative way, it will keep our optimism high which keeps us healthy. And we must teach our people it is very important to be optimistic about life.

Dorothy Mae Pickens Jenkins

Amplified Bible (Zondervan)

John: C7, V6
6) Whereupon Jesus said to them, My time (opportunity) has not come yet, but any time is suitable for you and your opportunity is ready any time always here].

Philippians C3, V13
I do not consider, brethren, that I have captured and made it my own

[yet], but one thing 1 do [it is my one aspiration]: forgetting what lies behind and straining forward to what lies ahead,

Philippians C4, V6, & V10

6) Do not fret or have any anxiety about anything, but in every circumstance and in everything, by prayer and petition (definite requests), with thanksgiving, continue to make your wants known to God. 10) 1 was made very happy in the Lord that now you have revived your interest in my welfare after so long a time, you were indeed thinking of me, but you had no opportunity to show it.

Common Sense

In Mrs. Mabel's day versus today's society, competing is more challenging than it was back in old school days. We find that we don't only compete in our workplace; we must understand we have to compete in our love life. But we must learn we do have the ability and capability to draw love to us and also become successful human beings in our careers. But sometimes, the younger people in our society today commit too quickly to relationships. Not knowing how sometimes that person or persons are really feeling about them. It's similar to a family member's love; the norm is they should love us and show their love. But love doesn't always doesn't come from blood-related, and we are learning that's okay. Because it helps us to understand when they know the truth and the truth is not always easy to accept. But we want to feel accepted and love, so, therefore, we start to try and take care of our kinfolk needs and wants. And we become agreeable with them no matter what they believe is. We think it's our responsibility to do "so", because we are blood-related. And if we don't fall in line and follow their beliefs and accept their decisions, they will start to treat us very unfairly. And withdraw their love from us by treating us badly long enough, they will wear our will power down. And we want to be able to go on without them in our lives. Hopeful that our self-esteem is "shot", now we're feeling despair, and that's when they zero in on our vulnerability, within hopes of taking over our lives for ever and have us completely under their control. These people have a tendency to try to control everyone they come in contact with. And if we don't have righteousness, faith, and kindness within us, we will not have common sense enough to endurance it all. And in the meantime, not allowing them to walk all over us. Oftentimes these people are just wanting someone to love them, but they are afraid to reach out to someone for love. And they are afraid that if they do reach out, it will not be reciprocated back to them. And with the uncertainty that they already live with, it will become more than they can handle, and they don't want you to feel they need you. Because if that happens, then they can't work their plans on you the way they want. They will not show themselves in need of love because they think that's showing weakness on their part. And they dare not show anything but bravery because with that, they will be able to work their plan on you. Sometimes these people do let things go past the mental abuse and become physically violent. They want to be perceived to be decent upstanding human beings, but they often behave in an unacceptable attitude. Everyone has humility in them; it's just these people have only a sprout of humility in them. They only have a sprout of humility, just enough to keep themselves afloat. So they may keep being a throne on one's side ninety-five percent of the time they enjoy doing it. Rapidly trying to keep everything in perspective and at the same time making sure you remain insignificant to them. And the plans they have for you may look like you are of importance to them. In order to keep a healthy, kind relationship with these types of people, you have to set boundaries and live by them. Or you will end up in the clutches of their hands, and no matter which way you turn, you will not be able to get out. Without tearing your emotions apart, the situation is durable. But what I'm saying, why to go through that when you can use your common sense and your will, and the endurance of your faith will keep us well and safe from these sort of people. Don't let these people kill the love in you that you have for them and others who are in your life. Everyone needs love, don't let go of yours, or you will regret it. Keep the faith, and love will grow.

Dorothy Mae Pickens Jenkins

Amplified Bible (Zondervan)

Psalm: C55, V1

1LISTEN TO my prayer, O God, and hide not Yourself from my supplication!

BE MERCIFUL, and gracious to me, O God, be merciful and gracious to me, for my soul takes refuge and finds shelter and confidence in You: yes, in the shadow of Your wings will take refuge and be confident until calamities and destructive storms are passed.

Psalm: C59, V9

9) O my Strength, I will watch and give heed to You and sing praises: for God is my Defense (my Protector and High Tower).

Exodus: C34, V6

6) And the Lord passed by before him, and proclaimed. The Lord! the Lord! a God merciful and gracious, slow to anger, and abundant in

loving-kindness and truth.

Common Sense

Mrs. Clearview said, "We must learn how to use our instincts ability to source through different personalities and be accepting of others and their ways." We must have something approachable about ourselves; some of our instincts are inherited and some are developed by going through circumstance and maturing. Take your time to talk to people and get to know them; allow them to talk. I guarantee you will find out more about a person in minutes" then if you have spent "25 minutes" with them. You will know if they are a decent person or not and trust your instinct. This will stop you from making so many bad discussions before you start to mess up your life and anyone that listens to your messed up self. Go back to what I said in the beginning; instincts are very important. If we can't learn to have an instinct about others, we will not develop and learn how to use common sense and our own instincts about ourselves. Our instinct must become a skill for us; it's like becoming very good and exultant at what we have become.

Dorothy Mae Pickens Jenkins

Amplified Bible (Zondervan)

Proverbs: C9, V6

6) Leave off, simple ones [forsake the foolish and simpleminded] and live! And walk in the way of insight and understanding.

Proverbs: C3, V5, V6, & V13

Lean on, trust in, and be confident in the Lord with your heart and mind and do not rely on your own insight or understanding.

In all your ways know, recognize, and acknowledge Him, and He will direct and make straight and plain your paths.

13) Happy (blessed, fortunate, enviable).

Is the man who finds skillful and godly Wisdom, and the man who gets understanding [drawing it forth from God's Word and life's experiences].

Common Sense

Maeasia is in a very confusing relationship; she can't understand what kind of relationship she and India have. So it has come to Maeasia attention that she needs to identify her relationship that she has with India. Because they can't build a relationship if there is no understanding of one another. But there may be disagreements with each other, that doesn't mean the relationship can't work. It just means you have to learn each other's limitations and expect them. That's if the both of you want the relationship, but it can be very difficult, right, wrong, or indifferent. They have to decide whether its worth putting in the time and the work for it. And they have to be totally honest with each other, and they must learn to trust each other

But there again they have to put in the work, it's very time consuming So they had better give this some serious thoughts before pursuing it because it's impossible to have a meaningful relationship without trust. But it is a learning process, learning how to respect one another's shortcomings and agree to disagreement. And do not show a lack of understanding in each. Be there for each other in all of the needs of one another without deceit. Maeasia has given all she can give to the relationship; she is now in counseling just for this particular relationship. That has been going on for over a decade, and it looks as if the relationship is on its last leg. With no signs of improvement, but strange as it may seem, Maeasia thinks that is how India wanted it to end and feels that's what she wanted all along. And as Maeasia thinks back, there was a lot of indiscretion and deceit. That also left her believing she is a user and an abuser. But as much as it hurts Maeasia has accepted who India is, but they did not continue the relationship.

Dorothy Mae Pickens Jenkins

Amplified Bible (Zondervan)

Psalm: C101, V2, V3, V4, & V5
I will behave myself wisely and give heed to the blameless way-O when will You come to me?

Common Sense

I will walk within my house in integrity and with a blameless heart. I will set no base or wicked thing before my eyes. I hate the work of them who turn aside [from the right path]: it shall not trap hold of me. A perverse heart shall depart from me. I will know no evil person or thing.

Who so privily slanders his neighbor will I cut off [from me] he who has a haughty look and a proud and arrogant heart I cannot and I will not tolerate.

Alex is such an indecisive person; he usually is very careful in what he says and what he does. And he relies on who is in his life to set the foundation for what kind of relationship they have.

He is a manipulator, and honestly, that's part of who he is because he needs to build a good stable relationship. But he needs someone in his life that can make good, sound decisions because he doesn't trust himself to do so. And in the lifestyle he wants, he must be able to maintain it, so you see, he will always need someone to rely on. Because it's very difficult for this man to be without a significant other and continue to be able to go forward and obtain a normal successful life. He can and will eventually do so, but it's just going to take a lot of time and struggle to get there. That's why in his mind, he needs a spouse who is very smart. He is a very smart intellectually man, but when he is going through hard times, he relies on his charm and devotion. The woman that's in his life, in his mind, he can't do this without her. Because he doesn't have the stamina to go through this alone again.

Dorothy Mae Pickens Jenkins

Amplified Bible (Zondervan)

Proverbs: C3, V26

26) For the Lord shall be your confidence, firm and strong, and shall keep your foot from being caught [in a trap or some hidden danger].

Proverbs: CB, V35

35) For whoever finds me [Wisdom] finds life and draws forth and obtains favor from the Lord.

Proverbs: C11, VI

FALSE balance and unrighteous dealings are extremely offensive and shamefully sinful to the.

Lord, but a just weight is His delight. {Lev19:35, 36: Prov 16:11]
Proverbs: C12, V9.

9) Better is he who is lightly esteemed but works for his own support

than he who assumes honor for himself and lacks bread.

Common Sense

Some men allow their insecurities to interfere with how they treat their girlfriends, fiancés, and wives. Now, this is not about intelligence, and most of us would think if a man wants to develop a good relationship with his significant other. He should not be afraid to be truthful and sensitive to his true feelings for her. But most often, they don't reveal their true feelings because they are afraid to let her know in their mind. Because he thinks she will take advantage of him, but if he was thinking more clearly, he would know. That his intelligence would remind him it's not about his uncertainties, it's about pursuing someone for a potential relationship. And with that in mind, there is no way we can develop a healthy relationship if we don't have honesty But in the meantime, he wants her to be vulnerable to him and be accessible to his wants or needs. So he may seem to continue to be an impressive supportive man all on his own. But without her, he feels so alone although he's so self-absorbed in his own life. He forgets that his feelings for her is part of what he wants also, but he is just too afraid to admit it. And from the beginning, he knows his essential primary goal was to have someone very special that he cares about to be right there with him. To build a good life for himself, fall in love and grow in life together. And stay in each other's life for the rest of their lives.

Dorothy Mae Pickens Jenkins

Amplified Bible (Zondervan)

Exodus: C31, V3

3) And I have filled him with the Spirit of God, in wisdom and ability, in understanding and intelligence, and in knowledge, and in all kinds

151

of craftsmanship.

Philippians: C4, V13

13) I have strength for all things in Christ Who empowers me. I am ready for anything and equal to anything through Him Who infuses inner strength into me: I am self-sufficient in Christ's sufficiency.

Proverbs: C4, V13

13) Take firm hold of instruction, do not let guard her, for she is your life.

Philippians; C4, V23

The grace (spiritual favor and blessing) of the Lord Jesus Christ (the Anointed One) be with your spirit. Amen (so be it).

CHAPTER 11

THE POWER OF TRUTH

Common Sense

It is very hard for Dana and many other people to acknowledge the truth. Some people have a hard time admitting what the truth is and are often afraid of failure. They don't want to accept the consequences that come with it even though they know it's their fault. That's called not accepting responsibility, but what they really need is to grow a backbone on their own. And stop depending on someone else to make it and stop allowing others to take care of them. They complain about how they do it, when they are not willing to take responsibility and authority over their own lives. And stop "role" playing and taking serious actions to better their life. They may say they are going to take control, but sometimes that's all it comes to is a lot of words and no action. It's all verbal with no merits that we can't allow ourselves to become irresponsible.

That allows others in your life to be responsible for us, and that gives them some control over our life. And how we live may seem to be ok for a minute, but that becomes very annoying with a lot of anxiety. And it's your own fault because we allow ourselves to become irresponsible. Remember, self-preservation comes first with everyone, but then we should already know that since you have been irresponsible in the beginning. What we need to do now is put on your big girl pants, cut out the nonsense and start to act as if we have some kind of sense. You did get that, didn't you? I said "act" like we got some sense even if we don't feel like we work with ourselves. Haven't you heard the old saying, if you take one step, he will take two? Well, at least take that step, my child and keep in mind that you are his child. And you must know that if nothing else you have to know his children do not fail, you just have to know that, it's simply common sense. Mama grand would say, everybody has common sense. You just might have to dig a little deeper for yours; it's understood Just get your emotions in tack and don't allow yourself to become an emotional disgusting human being. And learning at this stage in our life we are not willing to put up with our own self. Because when you stop and look at everything, it even makes you sick. And if it makes you sick, how do you think someone else feels about all of that? Whether it's right, wrong, or indifferent, it's our life, and you need to clean it. Keep the truth in your heart, and it will flow through your body like "love". As our mothers said, love covers a multitude of troubles, but remember truth and self-preservation comes first. And the truth is we cannot take care of ourselves without recognizing the truth. We just need to know we have to walk with the peace of truth. And it will be impossible to fail and fall short of a successful peaceful life.

Dorothy Mae Pickens Jenkins

Amplified Bible (Zondervan)

Proverbs: C3, V6
6) in all your ways know, recognize, and know Him, and He will direct and make straight and plain your paths.

Psalm: C32, V5
5) l acknowledged my sin to You, and my iniquity I did not hide I said, I will confess my transgressions to the Lord l continually unfolding

the past till all is told]-then You [instantly] forgave me the guilt and iniquity of my sin Selah [pause and calmly think of that]

1 Peter; C3, V10 & V16

10) For let him who wants to enjoy life and see good days [goodwhether apparent or not] keep his tongue free from evil and his lips from guile (treachery, deceit).

16) [And see to it that] your conscience is entirely clear (unimpaired) so that, when you are falsely accused as evildoers, those who threaten you abusively and revile your right behavior in Christ may come to be ashamed [of slandering your good lives].

Common Sense

This young woman Summer is a spiritual soul, willing to tell the truth about many things even if it gets her in trouble. And there are not many like her, which kept her two steps ahead of those that were not truthful. As the old school saying goes, it is better to tell the truth than a lie because if you tell the truth, you will not have to have a good memory. Practice makes perfect in our world, and that puts her in a better place with us in society. Her power of truth made life easier for her to live successfully; she carries out the truth and lives by it. Her behavior and influence affects other people in a good way. You see, this young woman has a better chance at the probability of developing great opportunities for herself and others. But if she did not practice telling the truth, life could have been more difficult for her than it was. But to her belief, the truth worked for her, the free will of truth. This young woman is self-confident and self-sufficient in her adventure career. She is involved in helping people cope with their problems and everyday living in our society as a whole. And because she is so

155

truthful, that makes her a person better able to help others with their "truth". She tells you we cannot solve anything with a pack of lies You have to unravel all "lies" by telling the honest truth to resolve problems and find solutions.

The professional capacity that she works in has to be centered around good ethics, and she is only as good as her profession allows her to be. Because her main goal is to take care of her fellow human beings so they may live a better life by living the truth of it all. Her principle is if you are not willing, to tell the truth, she can't help you, which some would say she is too abrupt. But that would be a mistake of clarity because her philosophy is she must be stern to navigate the principle and behavior. So she may help them with accepting the truth of the matter. She has become one of the most extraordinary, kind, grateful, merciful person's that society will have the pleasure of knowing in her lifetime. This young woman is motivated by the righteousness of the truth.

Dorothy Mae Pickens Jenkins

Amplified Bible (Zondervan)

Job: C17, V9
9) Yet shall the righteous (those upright and in right standing with God) hold to their ways, and he who has clean hands shall grow stronger and stronger [Ps 24:4].

Psalm: C5, V12
12) For You, Lord will bless the [uncompromisingly] righteous [him who is upright and in right standing with You]: as with a shield You will surround him with a shield You will surround him with goodwill

(pleasure and favor).

Matthew: C5, V7, & V16

7) Blessed (happy, to be envied, and spiritually prosperous-with lifejoy and satisfaction in God's favor and salvation, regardless of their outward conditions) are the merciful, for they shall obtain mercy!

16) Let your light so shine before men that they may see your 'moral excellence and your praiseworthy, noble, and good deeds and recognize and honor and praise and glorify your Father Who is in heaven.

CHAPTER 12

INSECURITIES AND LACK OF SELF-CONFIDENCES

Common Sense

Mrs. Beasley has problems dealing with people of her kind; they are so consumed with their own problems. They are not equipped to handle any situations that could normally be made under normal conditions. But they are so complexed they are not in an appropriate mindful condition to make good decisions concerning themselves and surely not others. So that is why they usually keep to themselves so they will not hurt others and not know they did. They are so afraid of hurting others they would just refuse to be in a relationship of quality. So there will not be any possibilities of hurting anyone or getting hurt. And so they promise themselves they would not be a good enough friend for the relationship right now, and it could be something they would come back to at a later date. When they think that they are more equipped to maintain a healthy relationship with others. Regardless of whether it turns out for the best or not, it seems like that is the best decision they could make at the time without getting hurt or hurting someone else. They are so troubled they only have enough energy to carry themselves, and even at that, it seems to be at risk. But at least they are feeling thankful for not involving someone else in this mess. When sometimes that's not true at all, others still become hurt; it's just a risk some of us take, and in the end, we make the best of it. But sometimes professional help is needed to carry them through. We cannot put ourselves in the position to go through stuff along; remember that's our professionals' job is to help us through our problems. Providing we allow them to, yes, it's a lot of work, but if we follow the procedures, it will keep us from quitting on ourselves and our relationships. We can work through circumstances easier if we allow our professionals to help us and stop feeling like help is something we should be ashamed of. Please know if we refrain from trying to do it all our way and allow ourselves to accept help, our lives would be a lot better. And then we can start to treat ourselves and others better. It will be more pleasing to our human self. And favor will fall upon us and follow us the rest of our lives and our children lives forever. We must practice wisdom in our lives. It will help us to stay focused on what is good for everyone involved and keep all clarity

Dorothy Mae Pickens Jenkins

Amplified Bible (Zondervan)

II Corinthians: C2, V7
So [instead of further rebuke, now] you should rather turn and [graciously] forgive and comfort and encourage [him], to keep him from being overwhelmed by excessive sorrow and despair.

II Corinthians: C4, V8
We are hedged in (pressed) on every side [troubled and oppressed in every way] but not cramped or crushed, we suffer embarrassments and are perplexed and unable to find a way out, but not driven to despair;

II Corinthians: C1, V8
8) For we do not want you to be uninformed, brethren, about the affliction and oppressing distress which befell us in [the province of] Asia, how we were so utterly and bearably weighed down and crushed

that we despaired even of life [itself].

Jeremiah: C29, V11, & V13

11) For I know the thoughts and plans that I have for you, says the Lord, thoughts and plans for welfare and peace and not for evil, to give you hope in your final outcome.

13) Then you will seek Me, inquire for, and require Me [as a vital necessary] and find Me when you search for Me with all your heart [Deut4:29-30].

Common Sense

Janice has a sense of entitlement; this person is delusional with a disrespectful attitude. So you see, she has two marks against her already, no discipline about herself at all. She has an attitude as if the world and society owe her something for just being here. And in her mind, she decided all on her own she was going to do as she "wanted" and treat people as she wanted to. Whether it's right, wrong, or indifference, as long as she got her wants and her needs taken care of, she was fine with whichever way the cookie crumbles. She acted like she was out of touch with reality, and reality had no room in her vocabulary or life. Her deceit and deviousness with her self-righteous ideas led her to become envious. Which leads to strife, and with this kind of stuff in her, how could she develop any kind of decent, caring, loving relationship with anyone? Because after a while, all that turns to evil, and therefore she becomes an extremely demanding and unpleasant person. She becomes one of the most disagreeable, rude, and inconsistent people you would ever meet in your entire life.

But on the other hand, she could be a very creative and well-achieved person. But somewhere in her soul, she was hurting and feeling the

161

lack of something. Wanting to love, but didn't know how or even if she wanted it as if her thoughts were, it's not worth it. Because if her love wasn't returned in the way she thought it should be, she would not be able to sustain herself. She was always afraid that something unknown could come and destroy her wellbeing. So she had to keep an unfair controlling attitude, demanding rules on people and the things surrounding her world. And when she found that you didn't fit into her world anymore," she had no more use for you or any particular thing for you to do for her. The disrespect would arrive, and she would lash out, which after a time that left her very lonely and angry. Then that leaves room for depression to sit in, and it came in at an unfortunate time, which left her in an unsuccessful compromising position. And when she is not "good", she is not good for herself or anyone else. Because her senses start to tell her, someone or something is out to get her, and she must get her control belt out and tighten it up. Before she loses everyone and everything around her, including her mind, and using her emotions to trap someone for her benefit It was incomprehensible to her that the person or persons didn't see her way of doing things. She proceeded to do things her way to enhance the success and her wellbeing. She didn't understand that she can not build a healthy, successful life by making decisions straight off of her emotions. There is no way anyone can have a productive prosperous life in this society strictly off emotions that are irrationally thinking. And as we live "life" and make a life for ourselves, it has to be built on a solid, stable foundation; we have to become empowered. And not allow other people to control us.

Dorothy Mae Pickens Jenkins

Amplified Bible (Zondervan)

162

Psalm: C109, V2, & V3

For the mouths of the wicked and the mouth of deceit are opened against me: they have spoken to me and against me with lying tongues.

They have compassed me about also with words of hatred and have fought against me without a cause.

Proverbs: C5, V12

12) And say, How I hated instruction and discipline, and my heart despised reproof!

Proverbs: C22, V19

19) So that your trust (belief, reliance, support, and confidence) may be in the Lord, I have made known these things to you today, even to you.

Common Sense

Sam sometimes feels inadequacy in how others treat him, and that's a struggle for him sometimes. Because that gives others power over him, which allows others to manipulate him. But he is learning how to work on his inadequacy and not allow others to use that against him, which makes him stronger. And more independent of himself now, he finds himself more pleasing to himself than being preoccupied with what others are thinking of him. He decided not to allow himself to become a slave to his inadequacies because that will cause him not to live the successful life he had planned for himself. And take his place in society as a decent supportive, caring human being and not allow his inadequacies to define him. And sometimes, our shortcomings become our stronghold to make life better for us by not giving in to the weakness of it. And have more understanding for others which in turn makes us understand ourselves better.

Dorothy Mae Pickens Jenkins

Amplified Bible (Zondervan)

Job: C26, V3

3) How have you counseled him who has no wisdom! And how plentifully you have declared to him sound knowledge!

Job: C36, V5

5) Behold! God is mighty, and yet despises no one nor regards anything as trivial: He is mighty in power of understanding and heart.

Job: C37, V23, & V24

Touching the Almighty, we cannot find Him out; He is excellent in power: and to justice and plenteous righteousness He does no violence. [He will disregard no right][I Tim 6:16].

Men therefore [reverently] fear Him: He regards and respects not any who are wise in heart [in their own understanding and conceit] [Matt 10:28].

Common Sense

Bison can not stand rejections unless he is the one doing it, somewhere in his childhood. Someone had done something that was unkind to him, so he took it to heart and started to feel rejected. And he starts to dish out rejections to others before they would do it to him so that he may feel safe from being rejected. Someone else has forced their unfavorable desires on him, a helpless child, because that's not what our society needs in this world. That is not the kind of behavior that

164

anyone needs in their life while growing. Most often, it carries over into their adult life and interferes with their self confidences, and allows them to doubt themselves. As a hold, there is no valve in rejection; it tends to cause dismissal of healthy emotions and affections. He is keeping his hurt and pain so deep inside until it starts spinning out of control. His feelings currently do not allow him to know he's hurting others. Because he was violated as a child left him with an unhealthy balance of emotions.

Dorothy Mae Pickens Jenkins

Amplified Bible (Zondervan)

Ephesians: C4, V14 & V19

14) So then, we may no longer be children, tossed [like ships] to and fro between chance gusts of teaching and wavering with every changing wind of doctrine,[the prey the cunning and cleverness of unscrupulous men, [gamblers engaged] in every shifting form of trickery in inventing errors to mislead.

In their spiritual apathy they have become callous and past feeling and reckless and have abandoned themselves [a prey] to unbridled sensuality eager and greedy to indulge in every form of impurity [that their depraved desires may suggest and demand].

Psalm: C66, V20 &V18

Blessed be God Who has not rejected prayer nor removed His mercy and loving- kindness from being [as it always is with me.

18) Ill regard iniquity in my heart, the Lord will not hear me, [Prov15:29:28:9: 1:15: John

CHAPTER 13

THE RESOURCES AND ABILITIES TO OBTAIN

Common Sense

Mrs. Bailey said we will never be without something we need, but if so, it's only for a little while Because you can always get material things back easily But it's not so easy when it's a person that you think you want or need back in your life; that's a bit more challenging. But with endurance and careful planning, we can develop the abilities to use all our resources to obtain it. And go on with our lives and establish ourselves to live a full, happy life. Stop allowing yourself to put yourself last in your life, put yourself first. Stop deceiving yourself to the fact that this person wants you. When you know, you should be determined to make wiser decisions for yourself than what you have been doing. Stop putting yourself out there to be used at his desire. And when his appetite changes, he's already sought out another something or someone to claim his desires, whether you agree with it or not So you see, we should already know self-preservation comes first, don't be so determined that you leave yourself in need. Because he is certainly not going to be in need of anything for himself. He will use any means necessary to take care of his needs and all of his little insignificant requirements. Our requirements are very significant because we are very determined, but we fall short in making him understand that.

Simply stop allowing him to take us for granted whether we want to or not. Know that we are worthy of his attention and kindness if he doesn't give it Just ask yourself if we can take care of yourself better than anybody can. And if he is not going to comply, then what do we need him for? To be determined but just be determined on what is right and what is right for our life. Yes, we should honor our men, but they should hold us in that same respect. And then both people will automatically honor one another in all circumstances because that is the right thing to do.

Dorothy Mae Pickens Jenkins

Amplified Bible (Zondervan)

Proverbs: C14, V33

33) Wisdom rests [silently] in the mind and heart of him who has understanding, but that which is in the inward part of [self-confident] fools is made known 32,6].

Proverbs: C2, V20, & V7

20) So may you walk in the way of good men, and keep to the paths of the [consistently] righteous (the upright, in right standing with God).

7) He hides away sound and godly Wisdom and stores it for the righteous (those who are upright and in right standing with Him): He is a shield to those who walk uprightly and in integrity.

Proverbs:C1 V23

23) If you will turn (repent) and give heed to my reproof, behold I [Wisdom] will pour out my spirit upon you I will make my words known to you 11:2, 1:17-20].

Common Sense

Paige said let us not be ignorant to the rules of life, by choosing not to listen. Choosing to listen will enhance our confidence. To be assured that we will understand how our society works, whether it is personal, or business. We must be ethical and intelligent enough to listen. So we may become educated, having the understanding to keep our minds interested in wanting to learn, and be of good rapport.

Dorothy Mae Pickens Jenkins

Amplified Bible (Zondervan)

Hebrews: C5, V8

8) Though he were a Son, yet learned he obedience by the things which he suffered.

Isaiah: C1, V17

17) Learn to do well, seek judgement, relieve the oppressed, judge the fatherless, plead for the widow.

Deuteronomy: C4, V10

10) Especially how on the day that you stood before the Lord you God in Horeb, the Lord said to me Gather the people together with me and I will make them hear My words, that they may learn [reverently] to fear me all the days they live upon the earth and that they may teach their children.

Deuteronomy: C31, V12

12) Assemble the people-men, women, and children, and the stranger and the sojourner within your towns-that they may hear and learn

[reverently] to fear the Lord your God and be watchful to do all the words of this law.

Common Sense

MrTy said, "Use your wit and don't feel an obligation to your circumstances." Keep your faith, love, compassion, concerns and attention to what is going to work for you and your family I know we don't understand how we will stretch this paycheck this month. That's when you put your wit into action and let common sense withstand the hardship.

Dorothy Mae Pickens Jenkins

Amplified Bible (Zondervan)

Psalm: C40, V1
1) I waited patiently for the Lord, and he inclined unto me, and heard cry.

Proverbs: C3, V3
3) Let not mercy and truth forsake thee, bind them about thy neck, write them upon the table of thine heart.

Psalm: C19, V8
8) The precepts of the Lord are right, rejoicing the heart, the commandment of the Lord is pure and bright, enlightening the eyes.

Proverbs: C23, V4
4) Weary not yourself to be rich: cease from your own [human] wisdom [Prov 28:20: 1 Tim 6:910].

Common Sense

Mrs G Cowands said, "Happy means a perfectionist, and she wants perfection for us." Trying to live faultless lives, taking us through life trying to live righteously. Working toward being perfect that will bring us to peace. Peace will allow love, mercy, affection, kindness, strength, and passion. And pleasing pleasures will flow through our body with love in our hearts for one another.

Dorothy Mae Pickens Jenkins

Amplified Bible (Zondervan)

Proverbs: C17, V22

22) A happy heart is good medicine and a cheerful mind works healing, but a broken spirit dries up the bones.

Proverbs: C3, V13

13) Happy (blessed, fortunate, enviable) is the man who finds skillful and godly Wisdom, and the man who gets understanding [drawing it forth from God's Word and life's experiences].

I Kings: C10, V8

8) Happy are your men! Happy are these your servants who stand continually before you, hearing your wisdom.

Psalm C128, V2

2) For you shall eat [the fruit] of the labor of your hands, happy (blessed, fortunate, enviable) shall you be, and it shall be well with you.

CHAPTER 14

CONSEQUENCES OF USING DRUGS

Common Sense

Mrs. Mindy said, we know if we drink stagnant water, we will become nauseous, sick and could possibly die. But that is not the only thing that could happen, it can become unfavorable and influences our mind, and our minds become contaminated. And changes your lifestyle from a decent person to not being able to handle relationships with family and friends. And even strangers and the effect of it can be so bad it will affect husbands, wives, significant others and your business relationships. And they will have such a stagnated mind, they will know in their heart they have become this stagnated person, but they don't care anymore. Because they have allowed themselves to become enjoyable by trying to make other people's lives like theirs. They are so envious of you they tried to suck your valves right out of our soul. Whether we were just ignorant or all had a college degree, it would not make any difference. But if you would have just let them talk, they would have told you everything you wanted to know. And even things you didn't want to know, if you didn't know any better, you would think this person is insane. They allowed themselves to drink something to ruin their lives and try to get anyone else that will listen to drink it also. They don't have common sense enough to know their hurting themselves, but it feels so good to them now they can't stop even if they wanted to. But remember that they really don't want to stop; that's why they enjoy doing it so much. Then their life ends in death, walking around on earth dead, running their stale water all over everybody they come in contact with. So how do you think you can teach anyone anything if you, yourself, don't have enough sense not to drink contaminated water. So ask yourself, where does that leave our children's future

Dorothy Mae Pickens Jenkins

Amplified Bible (Zondervan)

Numbers: C19, V17

17) And for the unclean, they shall take of the ashes of the burning of the sin offering, and the running water shall be put with it in a vessel.

Psalm: C71, V1 & V18

1) IN YOU, O' Lord, do I put my trust and confidently take refuge, let me never be put in shame or confusion! I have declared Your mighty strength to [this] generation, and Your might and power to all that are to come.

Titus: C1, V15

15) To the pure [in heart and conscience] all things are pure, but to the defiled and corrupt and unbelieving nothing is pure: their very minds and consciences are defiled and polluted.

Common Sense

Mrs. Mattie said, "Don't become a discouraged person; these kinds of people become frustrated with their lives, or just life period. They start to be depressed, delusional, and finally hopeless; that's when some turn to drugs." Now they are under the influence of drugs, so now they start to live a different life other than the so-called normal that society has shown us. Physiological drugs are now affecting their mind, and once the mind absorbs the drugs, they become not so normal anymore; it reduces the normal capacity of the brain. And the intensity has a great impact on the normal ability of how the mind works. So their total life changes and not for the better they don't have their typical life anymore. It's like the difference between a tuxedo and a pair of stone white wash jeans. By now, they can see their mind has been altered, so now common sense is trying to seep back in; if they keep drugging themselves, it is not goingto be an easy life for them. Or the people around them, now they have to try and make some good decisions for themself. Because this drug stuff is leading to destroying their lives, and if they keep this up, they will lose their children, home, and everything they own. Then the damage will be done, and they become impaired if they can't function. Did they lose their children, house, and everything they own? "Yes" because they allowed themselves to put drugs into their bodies and were not able to stop. I asked, "you", put your imagination to work. Can you see yourself in this predicament? And if you do, don't you know with your common sense and good professional help, you can rise above your mistakes. And become a caring, independent, successful healthy human being and give good back to our society instead of bad. And from going through such a mind-boggling, experience can't you see I am trying to bring understanding to us. If they had allowed professional help in their lives, they would "not" have had to go through such dramatic experiences. Now because they went through such dramatic difficulties now, they can see it is possible for a prosperous quality of life for the remainder of their life. And establish good powerful, successful lives and do not their your mind to become psychologically involved with the abuse of drugs. The morals of this story are don't do drugs because you just might not survive.

Dorothy Mae Pickens Jenkins

Amplified Bible (Zondervan)

Proverbs: C28 & V26)

26) He who leans on, trusts in, and is confident of his own mind and heart is a {self-confident] fool, but he who walks in skillful and godly Wisdom shall be delivered [James 1:55].

I Peter: C5, V7

7) Casting the whole of your care [all your anxieties, all your worries, all your concerns, once and for all] on Him, for He cares for you affectionately and cares about you watchfully, [Ps 55:22].

Proverbs: C10, V14

14) Wise men store up knowledge [in mind and heart], but the mouth of the foolish is a present destruction.

Job: C11, V20

20) But the eyes of the wicked shall look [for relief] in vain, and they shall not escape [the justice of God]: and their hope shall be to give up the ghost.

Common Sense

Chirssy recalls Mama grand talking about how to stay away from financial failure or troubles with financial ruins. As Mama grand frequently discussed the importance of recognizing you can't have everything you want instantly. Comprehend you can not spend all of your money and prepare yourself for the future. We must be conservative with our spending, use our common sense and stop spending and living above our means. If not, we will never become financially stable. And in our heart and mine, stop allowing ourselves to think our families should bail us out every time we get ourselves into financial difficulty. When we don't allow our self-confidence to work in our lives and take care of ourselves and family, that'sa lack of responsibility. It should become self-evident to us once this happens more than once or twice. All of us should take care of ourselves and our obligations. If we fail to do that, it is called a lack of self-respect. Self-restraint is what we should use in our everyday lives because that will enable us to keep our self-control and decency. And not think we are more important than our obligations and start preparing ourselves to endure and bring balance to every aspect of your life. How do I do this? As Mama grand said, "Use what has been given to you, use your common sense Stop partying, going out, shopping, and spending money as if you are a millionaire." Even millionaires go broke, grow old and have to live in poverty. And don't become confused and try to blame someone else for how you are forced to live because you didn't save for your future.

Dorothy Mae Pickens Jenkins

Amplified Bible (Zondervan)

Psalm: C27, V8

8) You have said, Seek MY face [inquire for and require My presence as your vital need] My heart says to You, Your face (your Presence}, Lord will I seek, inquire for, and require [of necessity and on the authority of your word].

Ecclesiastes: C7 V11

Wisdom is as good as an inheritance, yes more excellent it is for those [the living] who see the sun.

Job: C11, V12

But a stupid man will get wisdom [only] when a wild donkey's colt is born a man [as when he thinks himself free because he is lifted up in pride].

Proverbs: C16, V16

16) How much better It is to get skillful and godly Wisdom than gold! And to get understanding as to be chosen rather than silver [Prov 8 10, 19].

CHAPTER 15

EDUCATLON, DLSCIPLLNE, BEHAVIOR WILLINGNESS, AND KNOWLEDGEABLE

Common Sense

Becky knows empty is a word that can be used and means many different things. She remembered as a little girl growing up, her (Mama Grand) said I don't want you growing up empty-headed. Later she learned she meant, not using your common sense is being emptyheaded. Mama grand would say you were given common sense, use it for your good, not to act as if it is or was a preservative, as preserving my fruits for the winter. If you waste your time being empty-headed and living a foolish lifestyle, you are not appreciative of the valuable life gifts. Don't walk through life like an empty-headed chicken, pecking through life as if you don't know or have a clue about what life is. Mama Grand said, :I will not leave you here on this earth empty-headed; it is my job to make you realize you were born with common sense, and you are to use it and go after education." You can enable yourself to grow up in society and live and have ethical values, happiness, and successful life. She is saying that we must teach our children also to use their common sense and education together and make them a more level-headed person. So they may be able to deal with all aspects of our society.

Dorothy Mae Pickens Jenkins

Amplified Bible (Zondervan)

Ephesians: C5, V6, V11, & V15

6) Let no one delude and deceive you with empty excuses and groundless arguments [for these sins], for through these things the wrath of God comes upon the sons of rebellion and disobedience.

11) Take no part in and have no fellowship with the fruitless deeds and enterprises of darkness, but instead [let your lives be so in contrast as expose and reprove and convict them.

Look careful then how you Live purposefully and worthily and accurately, not as the unwise and witless, but as wise (sensible, intelligent people).

Ephesians C3, V16

May He grant you out of the rich treasury of His glory to be strengthened and reinforced with mighty power in the inner man by the [Holy] Spirit [Himself in dwelling your innermost being andp ersonality].

Common Sense

Mac, this young lady is a very attractive, sensible, reserved person. She never took her attractiveness as a sure way of getting what she wanted from life. She understood if she wanted a good healthy, righteous, professionally, successful life, it would take hard work. Good Godly common sense, along with her college degrees, so she may blend into yesterdays and today's society. She learned early on that she had to have some type of skill, education or college degree, to become successful in this world and blend into our society. She had to show so much braveness, courage and consistency in all that she set out to. There was no room for "failure"; she had very good communication skills. Never augmentation, disrespectful, disruptive, or give off bad vibes to make others feel she thought she was just a little bit better than the average person. Her vibes were always positive, and it is very unfortunate for those people that were not in her life. And they are not there now because they had no ethics or morals to appreciate a person of her quality. It seems this young woman's faith worked more in her life than the average person or persons. And people from all walks of life were very proud of her forthe way she lived and still is living a very Godly positive, successful life. And the people that are blessed to have her in their lives now know she is a lady of grace which was born in her, and some she learned and earned. By obtaining knowledge and making the right decisions for herself and her child. She was and still is a very honorable person to her mother and her elders.And has a very respectful, professional relationship with her associates and coworkers. This young woman is loved by all those around her. And why is that? Because she gives so much of herself and always left with plenty in reserve. Because that's the ingredients, she has in her, some born, some learned, some educational. And one of her greatest gifts she has given to everyone is common sense. If you have all or just half of what this young woman has, there is no way you can fail on anything you sit out to. The basics of this story is "love" and the "integrity" she has in her will equip anyone to become successful.

Dorothy Mae Pickens Jenkins

Amplified Bible (Zondervan)

Revelation: C2, V3
3) I know you are enduring patiently and are bearing up for My name's sake, and you have not fainted or become exhausted or grown weary.

Revelations: C2, V6
6) Yet you have this [in your favor and to your credit]: you hate the

works of the Nicolaitans [what they are doing as corrupters of the people], which I Myself also detested.

Proverbs: C1, V3
3) Receive instruction in wise dealing and the discipline of wise thoughtfulness, righteousness, justice, and integrity.

Galatians: C5, V22
22) But the fruit of the [Holy] Spirit [the work which His presence within accomplishes] is love, joy (gladness), peace, patience (an even temper, forbearance), kindness, goodness (benevolence), faithfulness.

Common Sense

Mary Janice is a vivacious woman that knows where her life is going and how long it's going to take her to get there, with or without him. She is well educated with common sense; she not only has "common sense", but she also utilizes it, right along with her education. "Yes" she is married, the husband is a little "Insecure," but not to the extent that they can't fix it if they really put some hard work into it. The problem is both people have some growing to do if there is only one of them trying to do all of the work. I will tell you right now, it is not going to work. They need the help of a professional to pull this marriage back together, so they may be able to start working on how they can fix this. And stop acting like they don't know what they have to do, but she or he just don't want to put in the hard work to get it "done". So what they did is stop mentally fighting and start using their common sense along with the help of a professional counselor. And stay together, living a successful prudent life, and learning to use their wisdom.

Dorothy Mae Pickens Jenkins

Amplified Bible (Zondervan)

Hebrews: C13, V4

4) Let marriage be held in honor (esteemed worthy, precious, of great price, and especially dear) in all things. And thus let the marriage bed be undefiled (kept in dishonored): for God will judge and punish the unchaste [all guilty of seal vice] and adulterous.

Luke: C14, V20

20) And another said, I have married a wife, and because of this I am unable to come [Deut 24:5].

I Corinthians: C7, V8

8) But to the unmarried people and to the widows. I declare that it is well (good, advantageous, expedient, and wholesome) for them to remain [single] even as I do.

Psalm: V119, V99

99) I have better understanding and deeper insight than all my teachers, because Your testimonies are my meditation Tim 3:15].

Common Sense

Mama Grand said failure does not fit into our household; if we live life to its full potential, we can not fail or teach "failure." As Mama Grand said, I will not leave you on this earth empty-headed and useless. You can not live in this world and not develop skills; it's just not possible. Every one has capabilities that can turn into success, whereas unachievable is a lazy minded person, that has no mind to do

183

nothing.

The mind and body of these people work like a snail; in fact, its worse than a snail because we look at that part of our society as a spineless person without a backbone. That's why there is no room in this house for failures; it's simply not acceptable. We can not accept spineless people that don't care about themselves or anyone else. What we must do not become a spineless person; we must give our love, kindness and patients excessively. And learn to love, giving and teaching others to teach the same to everyone they come into contact with. So our society can start to heal from the slackers of the world.

Dorothy Mae Pickens Jenkins

Amplified Bible (Zondervan)

Hebrews: C10, V36
36) For you have need of steadfast patience and endurance, so that you may perform and fully accomplish the will of God, and thus receive and carry away [and enjoy to the full] what is promised.

Revelation: C14, V12
12) Here [comes in a call for] the steadfastness of the saints [the patience, the endurance of the people of God], those who [habitually] keep God's commandments and [their] faith in Jesus.

Psalm: C19, V9
9) The [reverent] fear of the Lord is clean, enduring forever: the ordinances of the Lord are true and righteous altogether.

Deuteronomy: C31, V6

6) Be strong, courageous, and firm: fear not nor be in terror before them, for it is the Lord your God Who goes with you: He will not fail you or forsake you.

Common Sense

Mrs. Sadie said, "We should feel very fortunate to be breathing and know, there is hope. There is always hope for a better life for ourselves, the children and all generations." Mama Grand said, "My dear sweet child, all of us must know, if you have hope, we will always have enough courage to endure wherever life takes us." I once knew a man who said that hope will never lead you anywhere you can't go. Hope is when we watch our children grow up and go out into the world and not be physically harmed or get their hearts so broken beyond repair. And so they may keep the love within them and passing the love on to their children and all generations. Hope is not being afraid when we are in the hospital lying in bed, with tubes going into our bodies and the doctors and nurses telling us we need to shut our eyes and rest. And trust them to take care of us; that's what hope is. Hope and trust in the doctors and nurses, to keep hope alive in us, we must clothe ourselves in mercy and love.

Dorothy Mae Pickens Jenkins

Amplified Bible (Zondervan)

Psalm: C27, V14

14) Wait and hope for and expect the Lord: be brave and of good courage and let your heart be stout and enduring. Yes, wait for and hope for and expect the Lord.

Psalm: C33, V18

18) Behold, the Lord's is upon those who fear Him[who revere and worship Him with awe], who wait for Him and hope in His mercy and loving-kindness.

Romans: C15, V13

13) May the God of your hope so fill you with all joy and peace in believing [through the experience of your faith] that by the power of the Holy Spirit you may abound and be overflowing (bubbling over) with hope.

Psalm: C16, V11

11) You will show me the path of life: in Your presence is fullness of joy, at Your right hand there are pleasures forevermore. [Acts 2:25_28, 31].

Made in the USA
Monee, IL
03 July 2021